HEALING A COWBOY'S HEART
Cowboy Dreamin' 2

I0520399

Sandy Sullivan

Erotic Romance

Secret Cravings Publishing
www.secretcravingspublishing.com

A Secret Cravings Publishing Book
Erotic Romance

Healing a Cowboy's Heart
Copyright © 2013 Sandy Sullivan
Print ISBN: 978-1-63105-007-7

First E-book Publication: August 2013
First Print Publication: December 2013

Cover design by Dawné Dominique
Edited by Stephanie Ballestreri
Proofread by Mahalia Levey
All cover art and logo copyright © 2013 by Secret Cravings Publishing

PUBLISHER
Secret Cravings Publishing
www.secretcravingspublishing.com

Dedication

To all the cowboy lovers out there. This is for you.

HEALING A COWBOY'S HEART
Cowboy Dreamin' 2
Sandy Sullivan
Copyright © 2013

Chapter One

"What the hell?" Jeffery Young slammed on the brakes and pulled his beat up Chevy truck over to the side of the road.

"Where we goin', Daddy?"

"To the south pasture, but I need to figure out what these people are doin' on our land, buddy. You stay here." He hopped out of the truck but left it running to keep it cool in the interior for his son. Three-year-old Ben loved to go with his dad on ranch business. Even though summer had officially come to an end, the days still got hot in Bandera, Texas. Today they'd planned to check on the water trough in the south pasture. He needed to patch it before winter set in.

"Okay," Ben said, swinging his small booted feet.

Jeff hopped out of the truck, slamming the door behind him. "Who the hell are you? What are you doin' on Thunder Ridge land?"

A petite blonde stood next to a larger guy he recognized from the land surveyors office in town. He noticed right away how her hair caught the sunlight, bouncing it off the curls when she turned to face him. Green eyes the color of spring grass gazed at him behind the small round glasses perched on her nose.

"Excuse me?"

"What are you doin' on my land?"

"Surveying. What does it look like?"

The woman sounded way too damned perky for his taste. "Who are you?" He turned to face the man from town. "George, what's goin' on here?"

"We're doin' a land survey, Jeff." George motioned to the woman next to him. "This here is Terri Kennedy."

"Nice to meet you." She held out her hand, but he ignored it with a scowl.

"No one ordered a survey of our land. You don't need to be on our property."

"It's not for Thunder Ridge. It's for the new development." George looked uncomfortable as he shifted back and forth on his feet.

"Get the hell off my property," Jeff snarled. "We ain't supportin' the developers takin' over the ranch land out here."

"We have a right to use this road to survey the property boundaries. It's a county road."

"Not as long as you're off the blacktop, it ain't. It's Young property."

"Is he correct, Mr. Scott? Is this private property beyond the blacktop?"

"Yes, ma'am."

"Well then, we shall move to the blacktop area." She stomped her booted feet as she moved twenty feet up the road. Her curvy little ass bounced with each step, emphasizing the cute roundness much to his chagrin. "Now, we can continue where we left off. I'm sure you can make the adjustments to the measurements."

"Yes, ma'am."

The little smirk on her kissable lips drove his anger higher. He didn't want to notice anything about the woman, but here he stood watching everything about her. "Fuck."

"Did you say something?"

"No, ma'am. Get your business done and get off this road."

"You know you don't have to be so surly. I'm not doing anything wrong. I'm here as the architect for Meyer, Jessup and Cole."

Jeff moved closer. Something about her pissed him off. Was it the development or her in general? He didn't care. She needed to leave and leave fast. "Whoever they are."

"They are the firm handling the land development in this area."

"We don't want a damn development here. We have plenty of problems with not enough open land for the wildlife around here. Having houses will take away the natural habitat."

"I'm sorry, sir, but there isn't anything I can do about it. I'm only here to make sure the surrounding property the developers bought will be able to handle the architecture they are planning to build."

"Just get done and get out of here. If you ain't gone before I get back, I'll have you arrested for trespassin'."

"Try it, buddy! We aren't on your property now."

"You *were* lady," he growled, spinning on his booted heel and heading back to his truck. "Damn infuriatin' woman. Who the hell does she think she is? This is our property. She doesn't belong out here in her fancy shit-kickers, her designer jeans or her fancy western shirt. Like her outfit would make her fit in. Ha!"

"Daddy?"

"Yeah, buddy?" he asked, trying to calm his temper. The last thing he wanted was Ben thinking he'd gotten pissed off at him. His mother did enough damage when she had him to last a fucking lifetime.

"How come we missed the cake at Grandma's? I wanted cake."

"We'll get some when we get back, okay? I didn't think a wedding reception was a good place for you." It wasn't the whole truth and he knew it. He'd taken the easy way out of watching Joel and Mesa cut their cake. The wedding was beautiful, but he just didn't want to see his brother happily simpering over his new bride when his bitch of an ex-wife didn't even spend their wedding night with him. She went off with her friends, got drunk and disappeared for two days while he frantically tried to find her. He should have known from day one what kind of life they would have, but he didn't want to realize she wanted only his family's name and the prestige of the ranchland they owned. "Grandma will save you some, I'm sure."

"Okay."

He glanced at his pride and joy. Even if he hated his ex, at least she'd given him Ben. He loved the kid with everything in his heart. His boy was turning into a miniature of himself from the tip of his straw cowboy hat to the belt buckle he insisted on wearing. The kid was cowboy to the bone. No doubt about it. Not like he had much choice since all eight of his uncles were cowboys and so was his granddad. They ran Thunder Ridge Cattle Ranch including the small dude ranch they'd turned the place into to supplement their income.

He took his job of feeding his pony to heart too. Every morning they went out to the corral behind the main house, fed and watered the small horse before any other chores were done.

"Let's get this done then so we can go back for the cake."

"Yep."

Jeff glanced in the rearview mirror only to catch the woman watching him pull on down the road.

* * * *

Terri shielded her eyes from the glaring sun as she watched the man slowly pull down the road. She noticed his long, lean frame when he'd climbed out of the cab of his dirty, old truck. He definitely had cowboy down to an art from the top of his cowboy hat to the tip of his dirty boots. She could tell he was the real deal unlike the men she knew in Houston. Even though Houston was smack dab in the middle of cowboy country, most men she dated weren't cowboys. They were strictly corporate types—suits, ties and penny loafers.

Too bad she couldn't see his eyes. You could tell a lot about a man by his eyes.

Oh well, he'd been so pissed off at her being there, it's not like he would have looked twice at her anyway. She glanced down at her outfit. The new jeans, western shirt and pointed toe cowboy boots looked cute this morning when she'd put them on, but up against his tattered jeans, plain blue T-shirt and worn boots, she looked like a city slicker. Not something she wanted. She needed to fit in according to her clients. She had to rethink her clothing choices apparently.

Getting in with the locals was a priority. She needed information on the water levels, plants, wildlife and other pieces of the puzzle to be able to put together the plans for the housing development, and who better to get it from than one of the local cowboys.

She looked at George wondering whether she could get the information from him. Nah, he seemed like a nice enough guy, but he wouldn't have the ins and outs knowledge of a cowboy. Hmm. Maybe she could stay at one of the local dude ranches and pick the brains of the wranglers. Yeah. Sounded like a good idea to her.

"Hey, George. I know there are several dude ranches around here. Which one do you think is the best?"

"Thunder Ridge."

"Like the one that belongs to the cowboy who just chased us off his land?"

"Yep." George spit tobacco juice several feet away.

Totally gross!

"It's the nicest in the area. They have a great main lodge, meals are included, swimmin' pool. You name it. They got it. The small little guest cabins are the best, although I hear there are ghosts in the main lodge."

"Really?"

"Yep." He scratched his chin. "One of the boys just got married this weekend to a city gal from Los Angeles."

"Boys?"

"There's nine of them out there, including Jeff who you just sort of met. He's kind of testy, that one. Doesn't take kindly to strangers on their property. He's been very vocal about hatin' the land developers buyin' up the property out here."

"I gathered that."

"He's got a real piss pour attitude about him these days. 'Course with his ex bein' such a bitch, I can certainly see why."

"Hmm."

"You could do worse than goin' out there for a few days if you're thinkin' along them lines."

"I was, yes. I need more information."

"Get in good with one of them boys and you'll have everythin' you need. The family has been here for a long time. Those boys grew up here. No one knows the land like they do."

"Thank you for the information, George. You've been a big help." She glanced at the sun making a slow decent into the evening sky. "Are we about done here?"

"Yes, ma'am. Just figuring up the last of it. I'll get the stakes posted tomorrow so you all know where to cut the parcels."

"Thank you. You've been a huge help."

"You're welcome, ma'am."

George packed up his gear a few moments later before they headed to where his survey truck sat on the side of the road.

Oops. They hadn't moved the truck. It still sat on Young property. She snerked. *I should have George put one of the survey stakes right there since it's on the dirt road. Really piss off Mr. Jeff Young, the jerk.*

She could see dust billowing in the distance. "We'd better get out of here. I think our non-hospitable company is coming back. I don't know about you, but I don't want to end up in jail."

"Jeff is a lot of talk. He wouldn't call the cops since he doesn't want to have to deal with the sheriff."

"Oh?"

"Yeah. The sheriff is who his ex cheated on him with. They don't have much to do with each other if they can avoid it."

"Oh. I can see why he wouldn't."

"Yep, but we should be goin' anyway. You don't want to rile the Young family. You could use them on your side if you're set on puttin' in them houses you're plannin'."

"Thanks. Let's get out of here, then."

George started the truck just as Jeff pulled alongside his vehicle, slowing down to glare at them from inside his own.

Damn, the man is a jerk! What an ass!

George rolled down the window when Jeff rolled down the passenger window of his. "We was just leavin', Jeff."

"See that you do, George. I don't wanna see her back out here."

Terri saw a cute little boy wave from the passenger seat and she waved back. "Cute boy."

Jeff glared before gunning his truck, fishtailing slightly until the truck found pavement.

"Is he always so personable?"

George chuckled. "Yep. Wait until you get to know him a little better. It's even worse when you're close to him. He's always gettin' into fights with his brothers over somethin'."

"Sounds like a charming family."

"Oh, they're nice enough, especially Nina. She's his momma. Nice lady. Her sister works at the diner in town. Ann. She's sweet too. They just don't want to roll with the times. I'm surprised the ranch started takin' guests."

"Why's that?"

"They run cattle. Longhorns and beef cattle. Angus, I think. They're kind of stuck in the past, but I think they are working towards keepin' things more modern even though Jeff would live on the cattle alone. Unfortunately, beef prices have fallen on tough times over the last several years."

"I wouldn't see how beef cattle could survive out here. Or any cattle for that matter."

"Where'd you say you were from?"

"Houston."

"Well then you should know the story of the longhorns. They are a hearty bunch. I swear, they can live off nothin' for a hell of a long time. The Youngs have some great pasture land they cultivated over the years to be able to run the cattle on."

"Interesting."

"If you want to know ranch life, go stay out at their place."

"I think I will."

"Stay away from Jeff though. Talk to the other boys. They love the women, they do."

"Great. A bunch of bachelors, huh?"

"Yep, except for the one now. But a pretty woman like you should be able to get information out of them easy enough."

"Thank you for the compliment, George."

George shrugged and grinned a wide tobacco stuffed grin. "Just sayin'."

They pulled into the parking lot in front of the surveyor's office. George came around to open her door as she grabbed her briefcase and purse from the floor. "Thank you."

"You're very welcome, ma'am. I'll get things together and have the report for you by five tomorrow evenin' if that works for you."

"Perfect. I'm going to check out Thunder Ridge on the computer in my hotel room. I'll probably be stayin' out there by tomorrow evening so if you could, call my cell and leave me a message when it's ready."

"Sure." He tipped his hat. "Talk to you tomorrow then."

After a quick nod to George, she walked to her car and hit the key fob in her hand to open the back. She slipped her things into the trunk, then slammed the lid closed.

"Now for some dinner." The diner sat across the street from the surveyor's office. "Great. Maybe I can find out some information from the waitress at the diner. They usually love to talk and if she's relation to the owner's wife, she'd probably be more than willing to chat with me if I tell her I'm thinking of stay out there."

The bell over the door tinkled as she pushed it open. The place seemed quiet. *Great. Much easier to talk.*

"Take a seat anywhere."

"Thank you."

She found a booth near the back.

"What can I get you to drink?"

"Um, how about a Coke?"

"Sure. The menu is by the napkins there. We have meatloaf on special today with mashed potatoes, green beans and fresh bread."

"Oh, that sounds wonderful. I'll take it."

"I'll be right back with your drink." The waitress walked away as Terri studied her. Dark hair pulled back in a tight bun at the back of her head made her features sharp. Long straight nose and high cheekbones spoke of a Native American heritage somewhere down the lineage. The woman was stunning.

When she returned a few moments later with her drink, Terri asked, "Might you be Ann?"

"Yes'm. What can I do for you?"

"My name is Terri Kennedy and I'd like to know about Thunder Ridge Guest Ranch. Can you help me?"

"Certainly, sweetie. My sister and her husband own the place. You won't find a better time if you're lookin' for some real cowboyin' and ranch life."

"Great."

"You ain't from around here, huh?"

"How can you tell?"

"The clothes for one. You dress like a city girl, but you have a Texas accent."

"You caught me. I'm from Houston. I'm here on a little business, but I wanted some authentic cowboy exposure."

"You ain't gettin' it in Houston?"

"I live in the city. There are a few ranches around, but I wanted to see what the Hill Country cowboy ranches are like."

"You'll get in out there for sure."

"Sounds like a great recommendation."

The bell dinged behind the counter. "Be right back. Your dinner is ready."

Terri sipped on her Coke while she waited for Ann to bring back her plate. There were a few other patrons in the place, but they all looked like they belonged there. Wow, did she feel out of place.

"Here ya go."

"Looks fabulous, Ann. Thank you. Do you run this place all by yourself?"

"For the most part. I have a couple of girls who help during the rushes and the cook, but otherwise, it's mostly me. I worked the late shift today so I could be at my nephew's weddin' this afternoon."

"Oh, yes. George told me one of the boys out there got married today."

"George?"

Shit. I need to keep my big mouth shut if I plan to pass this off as a simple trip and not arouse suspicion. "Yes."

"Scott? The land guy?"

"He helped me out on the back road. I got stuck. He must have been out there doing some surveying or something."

"Seems we've had quite of bit of city folk gettin' stuck out on the back roads. Runnin' out of gas and such." Ann's eyes narrowed and her lips firmed into a straight line.

"Oh?" She needed to be careful or her cover would be blown before she got started.

"Yeah. It's how Joel met his bride. She ran out of gas back there near their ranch."

"How utterly romantic. The cowboy rides away with the girl on the back of his horse."

"Hey, Annie? Can we get some more coffee?"

"Hold your drawers on, Mick. I'll be right there." She glanced down at Terri with a smile. "Enjoy your dinner. I'll check on you in a bit. Holler if you need anything."

"Thank you."

"You're welcome."

The meatloaf melted on her tongue. She'd never tasted anything so good in her entire life. Within minutes, she's wolfed down her entire dinner and licked the fork clean.

"You must have been hungry," Ann said, bringing her another Coke.

"Apparently. You'd think I was starving or something, but you made the best meatloaf I've ever tasted."

"Thank you. My cook does most of the meal prep, but I still do a few things myself. The meatloaf is one of them."

"It's fabulous."

"I love someone who appreciates good food."

"My stomach loves you." She grabbed her wallet. "Here's a twenty. Keep the change for such fantastic service and food." With her purse in hand, she scooted out of the booth. "I've got a reservation to make for the ranch tomorrow night." She hugged Ann. "Thank you again. You've been great."

"You're very welcome. I hope you come by again before you head for home."

"Definitely! I wouldn't miss it."

Terri pushed open the door, catching the fragrance of lilies hanging in the baskets near the front of the diner. A cool evening breeze had worked its way up, bringing the temperature of the day to a tolerable level. Rain clouds threatened and she knew enough about the weather to know it would storm soon. She loved thunderstorms but getting caught in one in the middle of Texas Hill Country wasn't a great idea. Flash floods happened regularly although she doubted they had them in town. It was the outlying areas that had to worry more.

She drove her car to the small motel, which wasn't much, but it was clean and homey. She liked the room with its wrought iron bed, homemade quilt and fantastic lacy curtains. It reminded her of her grandmother.

As she opened the door, the cooler air of the room hit her in the face. Now, the temperature seemed almost cold. She quickly turned the thermostat down. *A bath would be nice.* Her suitcase lay open on the bed with all of the clothing she'd brought for her two week stay in Bandera. She might have to check out the western wear store in town to see if she could find something not so citified. They had faded jeans these days. Maybe she wouldn't stick out so much. She glanced at her boots. She needed to go walk in some mud with them or something. Scuff them up a bit so they didn't look so new.

Jeff's boots looked well worn.

"What the hell made me think of him? He's difficult, cranky, egotistical, and he's going to be a pain in my ass. I just know it."

She grabbed her pajamas before she headed toward the bathroom for a nice long soak. She'd even found some bubble bath in the bathroom when she's checked in so she could have bubbles, hot water…ah. Relaxing. She needed it after her week at work, the long trip from Houston to San Antonio in her car and being threatened with jail because of where she stood.

"Enough! I don't need to think of him. I'm sure I'll be dealing with him soon enough when I show up at his family's place. My stay should be interesting."

Chapter Two

The next morning Terri packed her suitcase, stuffed it into the trunk and headed back out to where she'd been the day before with George. The country was beautiful in the bright sunlight of the fall. Texas junipers dotted the landscape along with a multitude of rocks, brush and flowers. They sure had a different type of shrubbery than she had in Houston.

City blocks with its skyscrapers reaching for the heavens from every angle, left something to be desired most of the time.

She'd grown up in a small suburb of Houston and enjoyed the camaraderie of knowing her neighbors. Her high school had a small class and when she'd gone away to college in Houston, it had been a culture shock. The classes were huge. Teachers didn't know the students names and the campus stretched for miles.

The many years she'd spent studying for her architecture degree stretched on and on. Oh, she'd made friends, but it wasn't the same. She really wished some days, she had a close friend to just talk with, call on the phone or have lunch with.

She'd been working freelance for herself since she left her first job out of college two years ago. It was great working for herself, especially when she had a multi-million dollar account hanging in the balance like this one for the developers, but lately her existence seemed lonely, even to her.

At thirty years old, she really needed to quit jumping around so much. Her parents wanted her to settle down and raise a family, but she hadn't found the guy she wanted to settle down with yet.

She'd had a couple of boyfriends over the years too, but nothing serious. No one could live up to what she had in mind for her forever love. The man she had in mind had dark hair, pretty blue or gray eyes, a kick-ass smile and a killer body. He needed to be the same age as her or a little older. He'd have a great job. Some money saved. Maybe even a retirement plan.

A giggle escaped her mouth. Didn't she just have it all planned out even though she had no prospects of a boyfriend, much less someone to settle down with.

The gate to Thunder Ridge came into view. She hit the buzzer on the com when she drove up to the stone pillar.

"Can I help you?"

"Terri Kennedy. I'm a guest."

"Thank you."

The wrought iron bars slowly slid open. *Interesting.*

Several longhorn cattle grazed in the distance. A large home could be seen behind the trees as she drove up the long driveway. Several smaller cabins stood to the right when she pulled up in front of a three foot wall that separated the drive from the walkways. "What a cool set of buildings." A huge barn stood off to the back and she could see several cowboys walking around the corral. It looked like they were about to take a group of guests out on a ride. She'd have to take one while she stayed here. It'd been years since she'd been on a horse.

"Ma'am?"

A gorgeous looking cowboy stopped at her door. Dark hair framed his face and he had the most amazing blue eyes she'd ever seen. They reminded her of crystal blue water like you see in the pictures of the Caribbean. She opened her door. "Hello."

"Can I help you with your luggage?"

"I only have one suitcase, but if you'd like to grab it out of the back, I'll get my computer case. Thank you."

"My pleasure, ma'am."

"And you are?"

"Joshua, ma'am."

"Damn you make me feel old with the ma'am stuff."

He tipped his hat. "Sorry. It's part of how I was raised, ma'am."

"Thank God for cowboys," she murmured.

"Ma'am?"

"Oh, nothing." Joshua put her suitcase near the door of the car as she grabbed her briefcase and computer bag from the backseat. "Can you tell me where to check-in?"

"Yes, ma'am. I'll take you in there."

"Thank you."

She followed the gorgeous cowboy up the walkway to the side door made of wood. The damn thing must weigh a ton. He pushed it open and preceded her inside. "Follow me." They walked through what appeared to be a huge dining room with several wooden picnic type tables and one huge table at the front of the room. A staircase sat to the back leading up to what she assumed would be the guestrooms in the main lodge. *This is where George said they had ghosts.* She looked around quickly, but didn't see anything. *Stupid. Like they show themselves in the daytime!*

"Ma?" Joshua yelled. "I have a guest with me."

"I'm in the office."

"Follow me, please." He led her around the coffee station, through a large archway and into the hallway where she could see an office to the back of the room. "Here you go."

"Thank you, Joshua. I think I can handle it from here."

"All right. This is my mother, Nina. She handles the guest registration." Joshua set her suitcase against the wall.

"Terri Kennedy," she said, holding out her hand to shake Nina's.

"It's nice to meet you, Terri. Welcome to Thunder Ridge." Nina glanced at the card on her desk. "I have you in one of the outside guest cabins for a two week stay. Correct?"

"Yes."

"Great. I just need your credit card and we'll get your key." Nina glanced at Josh. "You can go back to work now, son. I can show Terri where she'll be stayin'."

"Uh, sure." Josh looked back as he walked down the hall and ran into the doorframe.

She giggled as he turned beet red.

"He's a good man. You seemed to have turned his head."

"Apparently."

"What are you hoping to accomplish while you stay here, Terri?"

Shit! Did she somehow find out about what I'm really doing here? "Just some hometown cowboying and ranch life."

"You have a Texas accent. Where are you from?"

"Houston."

"They don't have dude ranches there?"

"Well yes, but I wanted to come out to Hill Country and snoop around a bit. I'd love to talk to some of your sons about the cowboy way of life. I hear you have nine?"

"Ah yes, my sons. I'm sure they'd love to spend time with you. A pretty woman always gets their attention. They enjoy talkin' about ranch life."

"Perfect. I need to make some notes on different things about the ranch too. The soil, the water, the plants…you know."

"Really?"

"Yes. Um, I'm a conservationist."

"We have some very interestin' things on our land. I'm sure you'd love to explore. I could probably even convince one of the boys to take you out ridin' if you like to ride, so they could show you around the property."

"Absolutely, Nina. Thank you."

"We'll let you get settled in your room. Lunch is at twelve-thirty and dinner is at six. We ring the dinner bell outside and inside so you should hear it anywhere you are." Nina handed her the copy of her receipt and her key. "Follow me. I'll show you where your room is."

She followed Nina out the main doors and to the left. Two small cabins set off a little ways from the main lodge, each with two doors on them.

"Each cabin has two separate rooms that are connected by a door, but it will be locked between you and any other guests who

might rent the room across from you. It's empty at the moment."
They reached the door to the cabin. "I hope you'll be comfortable."

"I'm sure I will. Thank you."

"You're welcome. See you at lunch."

Terri opened the door so she could wheel her suitcase inside.
Glad she packed light, she hoped they had laundry facilities or
she'd be without clean clothes within a few days. The double-sized
bed took up most of the middle of the room with its wooden
headboard. The patchwork quilt was beautiful. Small bedside
tables graced each side of the bed and a small doorway to the left
looked like the bathroom. She'd have to check it out in a minute.
Against the wall sat a small couch which looked like it might pull
out into a bed too. The whole room would probably sleep four
adults comfortably. A small window looked out over the front yard
of the main lodge and the swimming pool. If the pool was heated,
she might partake of the water. She'd have to ask.

The clouds overhead promised cooler weather than the day
before. Fall in the Hill Country could be unpredictable with rain or
cold temperatures. The high today called for the seventies, which
suited her just fine.

She quickly put her clothes in the wooden dresser against the
wall, noting which ones needed washing. The more casual clothes
she's brought would probably suit out here better than anything
else she had. She might get away with not being called a city girl.

The lunch bell clanged in the distance, calling her to the main
lodge. She sucked in a ragged breath and blew it out on a sigh. It
was now or never.

She crossed the yard with slow, deliberate steps. Would he be
in there eating? She didn't know whether the family ate with the
guests or not. She hoped he wouldn't be because he would totally
blow her cover if he saw her.

When she opened the door, she was met with utter chaos or
what looked to be a chaotic area. A bunch of guests had gathered
in the room formerly empty. Probably thirty people stood in line to
get their lunch from the five people serving over the hot plates. She

swallowed hard looking toward the gathering of people as she slowly made her way toward the back of the line.

"I just love it here, don't you?" an older woman asked her friend standing in front of Terri.

"Oh yes. It's fabulous! Everyone is so nice. The cowboys are sweet as can be, but then again, it could be because we're old ladies. They were definitely taught their manners by their momma."

"She's a doll too."

"I think it's sweet how they all wait for the guests to get their plates before they get their own. It's nice that they have their own table, too, although I think it would be great if the cowboys ate with us."

The first lady giggled. "You just want one of those hunky youngsters to simper all over you, Marg."

"You're damn tootin', Liz. I may be old, but I ain't dead!" They both laughed as they approached the serving tables.

"Brisket, ladies?"

"Yes, please."

They went through the line chitchatting away like two little chickadees roosting on their nests. The two of them were too cute.

Terri looked down the long room and noticed the table with Nina sitting with a group of men. Younger men, except one older gentleman Terri assumed was probably her husband. The rest looked a lot like Joshua with one of them looking identical. Twins? *Wow.* She glanced around hoping to see Jeff so she could avoid him, but he didn't appear to be present. Had she gotten a reprieve? She hoped so. Now if she could avoid him for her whole two week visit, she would be thrilled. Somehow she didn't think she'd get so lucky.

The little boy who'd been in his truck sat next to Nina. He really was a cute kid. *Jeff's? Hmm.*

One thing she had noticed yesterday when they'd run into the infuriating man, he hadn't been wearing a wedding ring. George had mentioned an ex-wife who was a bitch, but he hadn't remarried or anything? Why she'd noticed was beyond her, but she had. Surely, she wasn't attracted to him?

Well maybe she was, but it wouldn't do any good. They were definitely on opposite sides of the spectrum. Her an architect with a firm trying to take the rangeland and turn it into housing developments and him a cowboy trying desperately to hold onto his way of life. She really couldn't blame him, but she was just doing her job, the one she'd trained for all through college.

The door creaked open at the end of the dining room. Terri glanced behind her to see Jeff come waltzing through the door looking like a cowboy of old. Dusty cowboy hat perched on his dark hair, western style shirt molded to his broad chest, dark worn jeans encasing his legs and dirty cowboy boots on his feet.

She quickly hid her face, turning toward the serving girl as she approached the hot tables. Jeff walked right past her without paying any attention to the people around him, although his cologne lingered.

The two older women sighed. "He's so standoffish. What do you think is his story?"

"I'm not sure. He's friendly enough when you talk to him, but he sure doesn't give anything besides polite conversation."

"He's the eldest you know." She waved her hand. "Of all the boys."

Terri continued to listen to their conversation as they made their way to the refreshment table to get coffee, milk or lemonade.

"He runs pretty much everything around here, but I think he tries too hard."

"The little boy is his from his marriage."

"He's a cutie."

"Yes he is, but the father? Sad case of being burned by a woman."

The women wandered off to a place to sit, while Terri kept her head down and moved as far away from the family table as she could to avoid Jeff. She'd eat and hole up in her room. Maybe she could find Joshua to ask about the things she needed to know or one of the other brothers although she didn't know their names.

Hopefully he would be working most of the time so she could get her research done. She bit her lip. She really needed to find out the answers to her questions. Unfortunately, he seemed to be the best one to ask being the eldest.

She ate her brisket while she kept a keen eye on him. Not that he was such a hardship to look at. He did have the cowboy thing down pat.

He touched Ben's head and smiled at him before he leaned over and kissed the boy on the head. Apparently, he cared a lot for his child.

Her heart skipped a beat. The man had a great smile, but obviously didn't seem to do it a lot. The family continued to chat amongst themselves.

She hoped Nina or Joshua wouldn't mention her.

She finished her food and pushed her plate away. If she got up to put her plate in the dirty dish bin now, he might see her. Maybe she'd wait until other guests were going up there. *Damn, avoiding him might be harder than I thought.*

Several other people went up to put their dishes in the bin so she took the chance and followed. She managed to put her plate in the tub, but when she turned to head back to the door to make her escape, her heart stopped when she heard Jeff raise his voice over the crowd.

"What the hell are you doin' here?"

* * * *

The last fucking person Jeff wanted to deal with tonight was his ex. He'd had a shitty ass day working in the south pasture on the water trough. Damn thing had sprung another leak after he'd fix the one yesterday. "What are you doin' here, Misha? I told you never to come out here without callin' first."

She pushed forward, headed for the door, past a blonde woman. "I need to talk to you."

"There's nothin' you need to say to me in front of my family and our son."

"Please, Jeff. It's important."

"Everything is important," he snapped, grabbing her arm to drag her into the main lodge area. Whatever she had to say, he didn't want said in front of the guests or his family. "What the hell is this all about?"

"I need a thousand dollars."

"What? Are you fuckin' crazy! I ain't givin' you any money."

"You will or I'll take custody of our son."

"Bullshit! We've been through this, Misha. We've already been to court and they gave me full custody. You have visitation. Nothin' more."

She yanked her arm out of his grasp. "I'll lie or whatever I have to do to take him from you."

"You bitch!"

"That's right. I'm a bitch. The same bitch you fucked, got pregnant, and then dumped the minute your dick didn't get what you wanted."

"I'll see you in hell before you get my son or any money from me. Now get the hell off my property before I have you thrown out of here on your ass."

"Is there a problem here, brother?" Jeremiah asked, standing close enough to Misha to intimate her from the shifting of her stance.

His entire family surrounded Misha and him. "I can handle her."

"You don't have to alone, Jeffery," Nina said, wrapping her arm around his waist. "You'll leave now, Misha, and don't bother threatening Jeff or Ben again. I'll mortgage this entire property to keep him from your clutches."

"We'll see about that!"

Misha pushed her way through the throng of people his family made up, stomping her way toward the door. She didn't even stop when Ben called, "Mama?"

Jeff hurried to Ben's side and picked him up. "It's okay, buddy. Mama had somewhere to be."

"She didn't even stop, Daddy."

"I know. I'm sorry." He hugged Ben tight as tears gathered in his eyes. *What the hell did I ever see in her?*

"Don't worry, son. We won't let her take Ben," James said, patting Ben on the head as he stuck his thumb in his mouth and laid his head on Jeff's shoulder.

God, I wouldn't know what to do if anything happened to Ben. The kid was his life. He was sorry every day for the hell Misha had put him through, but he wasn't sorry she'd given him Ben.

Maybe someday soon he'd find a woman he could tolerate long enough to get laid, but he sure wouldn't be able to handle one as a permanent fixture in his life. They are all too bitchy, self-centered, whorish, and didn't give a shit about the man or what his needs were. A man had the need to feel loved too. Not just used for the pleasure he could give a woman even though doing those things were pretty cool, they weren't everything.

"Why don't you take Ben in the kitchen for some ice cream?" Nina said, pushing him and Ben toward the double swinging doors. "I'm sure there are even some sprinkles in there."

"But, Ma?"

"Nonsense. He needs some Daddy time right now, Jeff. Go on."

"Thanks."

"You're welcome, son. Don't worry about her. She's all talk."

"I hope you're right."

He took Ben into the kitchen, found the scoop and the five gallon bucket of ice cream.

"Want some ice cream, buddy?"

Ben nodded before he wiggled to get down. "I love you, Daddy."

"I love you too, Ben."

After about an hour, they finished eating their ice cream, cleaned up the kitchen and he took Ben out to his truck to head for home. He hoped he didn't run into any guests. He didn't want to have to play nicey-nice with anyone tonight. If they could just run cattle on the place, he'd be a happy man. His parents didn't see it the way he did though.

As he walked out toward his truck, he noticed a blonde woman standing on the porch of one of the cabins the guests stayed in. From a distance, she looked familiar, but he couldn't quit place her. He shrugged. Didn't matter. He didn't mix with guests. He avoided them more times than not, unlike his brothers who liked schmoozing with them. His job was to take care of the cattle and keep the ranch running smoothly. Keep the stock fed. Keep everything from falling apart on the cattle side of the operation. If he did that, the rest of them could run the guest ranch into the ground for all he cared. He didn't like having people on the ranch playing cowboy, but he supposed the investment kept things in the black.

The woman backed away into the shadow of the porch. Odd. He shrugged.

"Let's get you to bed, buddy. It's past your bedtime."

"I don't wanna go to bed."

"Sorry. It's bedtime. We have to be up early to feed the horses."

"Okay."

Jeff opened the passenger side door on his truck and put Ben in his seat before he belted the boy in. When he went around to the driver's side, he glanced over his shoulder to see the woman again on the porch. He wondered for a moment why she seemed to be watching him, but he blew it off as a curious guest.

He drove up to his cabin a few minutes later. The place was home even though it didn't have a woman's touch. He didn't need it anyway. He liked his place just like it was. Roughhewn logs with a porch going around the front of the house. Two small windows overlooked the front yard he had fenced off for Ben to play in. He loved the small living room with the large fireplace gracing one wall and the kitchen where he had hoped one day a woman would love to cook for him and their children. "Bah! Women. They aren't worth the trouble."

He got a sleepy Ben out of his car seat and carried him inside. Within minutes, he had the boy stripped down to his Spiderman underwear, into his pajamas, and between the sheets on his bed. Ben snuggled down beneath his blankets.

"Night, Daddy."

"Night, buddy." Jeff turned off the lamp, but didn't leave the room right away.

Moonlight played on Ben's face coming through the window over his bed. His little boy. The tyke carried his dark hair and gray eyes, thank goodness. He was glad he couldn't see much of Misha in the child, but he knew she was his mother all the same and that chafed his hide.

If he would have listened to his brothers, he probably wouldn't have married her in the first place, but he hadn't. He'd loved her with all his heart. They'd told him she flirted and propositioned them for months before the wedding. Then when she'd disappeared right after the ceremony with her friends and didn't come home for two days, he should have realized what a mistake he'd made. Stubborn fool.

"I'm sorry, buddy. God, I wish your mama was someone else."

Jeff wandered out to the refrigerator and grabbed a beer. Damn, he needed to unwind before he tried to sleep. Dealing with his ex always soured his mood.

He tipped the bottle to his lips before he studied the clear bottle in his hands. The light reflecting off the golden liquid swirling around in the bottle reminded him of the woman he'd met yesterday. *Terri Kennedy. The sunlight reflecting off her hair looked like the beer in the bottle.*

"What the fuck? Where did that come from and why the hell am I thinking about her?"

He took another swig. *Her eyes were green like new grass in the pasture.*

"Huh."

He laid his head on the back of the couch as he remembered the woman standing next to George in her citified outfit. She was kind of pretty with her hair back in a ponytail and those wire rimmed glasses perched on the edge of her nose. He laughed a dry, not so funny chuckle as he rolled the cold bottle over his forehead. "I've been too damned long without a woman if I'm thinkin' about her." He took another long draw from the cold liquid. "She works for those fuckin' developers who are tryin' to take over all the property out here to make housin' developments out of them. Bring all those city folks out here to take over the land."

Grabbing the remote for the television from the coffee table, he flipped on the news just for some background noise. He didn't like the way his thoughts were roaming tonight. Women were the bane of his existence. Thinking about them just brought about heartache on his part. Look where Misha had gotten him. Miserable, that's where.

Terri didn't do anything to you.

"Terri? Why do I have to think about her?" He finished his beer. "She's out to destroy the whole damned place!"

"In more news. The firm working on the land developments in Bandera have hired Terri Kennedy, architect, to work on the particulars concerning environmental aspects of changing the landscape."

Jeff sat forward as the woman he'd seen out on their land came into focus on the television.

"Ms. Kennedy, can you tell us what plans you are working on at the moment?"

"We are studying the impact the development will have on the surrounding community, but rest assured we are planning to make the smallest changes possible and still get the housing project done. We don't want to affect the landscape at all if we can help it."

"Yeah right. They'll be fuckin' digging up trees, moving rocks and disturbing the wildlife the minute they fuck with anything."

"It's imperative that I talk to the local people to find out more about the area. I'm looking to get immediate feedback from the cowboys foremost since they work with this every day."

"Not from me, sister."

"How are you planning to get your information?"

"I'm staying at one of the local guest ranches in hopes of talking with the family and wranglers for my research."

"Which one?"

"I'd rather not say. My sources will be kept confidential except for in my report."

"There you have it, folks. Straight from the mouth of the firm's representative. It's a very controversial topic amongst the locals in Bandera since many would be affected directly by these housing developments. Several of the local ranches in the area don't want the development in, but there are a few selling out to them in hopes of a better life elsewhere. The weather has been particularly brutal this year with the lack of rain, making grazing especially hard. Many of the ranchers have given up. We haven't been able to get any of them to talk to us here at Channel Four News, but we'll bring you continued coverage as the story develops. Back to you in the studio, Marie."

"Thank you, Ashley."

Jeff flipped off the television before he set the remote back on the coffee table. Seeing the woman's face on the screen brought back the rush of anger he'd felt after meeting her the other day, but also something else. He remembered the slope of her neck, the curve of her shoulder and the shape of her hips. Why, he wasn't sure. She wasn't particularly pretty. Not a beauty in the model sense of the word, but she had something about her, a confidence maybe, that drew him to her.

"Doesn't matter." He stood to head into the bedroom. A nice warm shower would do him good before he tried to sleep.

With a touch of his hand, the light in the bathroom flipped on. One thing he did enjoy in life was a hot shower. Tonight he certainly needed it. He wrenched his shoulder this morning fighting with a particularly ornery calf who didn't want to come out of the brush even when its mama called to it. Some days he really hated his job, but most of the time he loved being a cowboy. Not like he'd known anything else in his life. Cowboying was in his DNA. He couldn't see his life any other way.

He quickly stripped out of his clothes and turned on the hot water. One thing he'd insisted on when his parents helped him build his house was a top of the line bathroom. The shower had tile from top to bottom along with a large rain showerhead.

With a weary sigh, he climbed in and shut the door. Hot water streamed down on his head as he closed his eyes. *God, that feels good.* He worked his shoulder under the heat of the water to try to loosen it up. He hoped it didn't stiffen up tonight while he slept, but he figured it would. *Some liniment might help.*

While he washed the dirt of the day from his body, his mind wandered to baser thoughts. It'd been several months since he'd been with a woman and even though he didn't need the headaches of a female in his life, he still had the needs of a man.

Maybe it's time to hook up with someone. I could do a bar run into San Antonio and probably pick up some chick there who wouldn't know who I am.

Terri Kennedy's green eyes popped into his head. She did have pretty eyes behind those wire rimmed glasses from what he could see.

He rubbed the soap over his cock and balls, losing himself in the feel of his hand over his flesh.

Would she be good in bed? How would she look with all of her blonde hair spilling over his abdomen while she sucked him off?

His eyes popped open. "Wow. Her?"

What the hell. He shrugged and closed his eyes again. *She's pretty enough.*

With his cock wrapped in his fist, he imagined her sucking the whole shaft between her lips. Each suck, each lick brought his desire higher. Her beautiful green eyes sparkled with lust as she sat between his thighs bringing him the best pleasure he'd had in a hell of a long time. Moments later, cum sprayed over his hand as he came so hard, he saw stars.

He slumped against the wall of the shower as he tried to catch his breath. It'd been a long damned time since he'd exploded like a sixteen-year-old kid with his first fuck. After he shook his head to clear his thoughts, he stood back under the water to wash the cum from his body. *Wow. That was pretty intense.*

Once he finished his shower, he shut the water off and grabbed a towel from the rack. He dried off before he wrapped the towel around his hips so he could head into his bedroom. Warm night breezes blew through the open window, sending goose bumps along his arms. Sleeping with the window open at night was one of his favorite things to do, along with hearing a women's sigh of completion. He rolled his eyes and shook his head. A woman was the last damned thing he needed.

Chapter Three

Sunlight filtered in through the window over Terri's head, bringing her out of her dreams gradually even though she didn't want to wake up. The gorgeous hunk of a man slowly licking her from head to toe had her desire at a peak. The moment she slowly came awake though, he disappeared like a wisp on the wind. She didn't even know who he was. His face had been shadowed in the dream. His dark black hair the only feature she'd been privy to see with any clarity.

Her whole body hummed with sexual tension. *God, I need to come.* It had been way too long since she'd had sexual gratification with anything other than her vibrator, but without a man in sight, she'd have to do this herself…again or do without…again. The clang of the breakfast bell echoed in the distance as she rolled over and looked at the clock. *Damn it! I over slept.*

She rushed to get dressed and pull her hair back out of her eyes with a ponytail holder. She didn't have time for makeup or anything else. *Not like I'm going to meet Mr. Tall Dark and Handsome at the breakfast table.* After she quickly slid her feet into her flip flops, she rushed out the door and ran smack into a broad chest.

Oomph.

"I'm sorry. I didn't see you."

"My fault, ma'am."

She glanced up into gorgeous blue eyes. "Joshua?"

"Jason, ma'am. Josh, Joel, and I are triplets."

"Ah. I can see the similarity, although I don't think I've met Joel."

"No, ma'am. He's off on his honeymoon with his new wife, Mesa."

"How great. I love weddings."

"Are you headed to breakfast?"

"Yes."

"May I escort you?" he asked, holding out his elbow. "I wouldn't want you to run into anyone else this morning on your way to get food."

"Well, thank you, kind sir."

"You're more than welcome, ma'am."

"Call me, Terri."

"Nice to meet you, Terri." They walked along the path headed for the main lodge. "I guess you're stayin' in one of the cabins?"

"Yes, for a couple of weeks. I'm doing some research."

"Research for what may I ask?"

"Rocks, brush, trees, animals of your native area for a uh…paper I'm doing."

"Interestin'. If you need some help, please feel free to find me. I'm usually around doin' one thing or another. Maybe I could take you ridin' so you can check out stuff."

"Good idea! Thank you. I'll see if I can find you after breakfast."

They started through the doors only to be almost run over by a racing three-year-old. "Whoa there, little man."

"I'm hungry, Uncle Jason."

"You shouldn't be runnin'. You know what Gran and your dad say. Besides, you about ran over one of our guests."

"Sorry." Ben dropped his head so she couldn't see his face. All she could see was the bent head with his little cowboy hat on.

Damn, if he wasn't the cutest little thing in his hat, jeans and boots. "It's okay."

"No. I'm not supposed to run in the house. I'm sorry."

"You're forgiven."

"Thanks." The kid spun around and rushed off toward the huge table at the end of the room where several more family members seemed to have gathered.

"Would you like to sit with the family?"

"Uh." She withdrew her hand from his arm. "No thank you. I don't want to intrude."

"No intrusion. We have special guests sit with us all the time."

She backed up a couple of steps. "No. Really. I see a couple of ladies I know. I'll sit with them."

"All right, then. Find me later and I'll hook you up with a horse."

"Thank you, Jason."

"You're welcome, Terri." He tipped his hat before he walked away.

Air rushed from between her lips in a heavy sigh. *Damn, these folks sure made a bunch of handsome cowboys.*

"He sure is a pretty one," one of the ladies from the day before said as they came up behind her in line. "What a nice smile too."

"Yeah, he really is." Terri couldn't help but agree.

"He's one of the triplets," the other lady added. "Can you imagine?"

"No," Terri replied. "I think one of those would be enough for me on even a fantastic day."

"I'd sure like to give it a whirl," the first woman replied. "I'm Marg, by the way. We didn't introduce ourselves to you yesterday at dinner. We're staying in the Annie Oakley room." She waved toward her friend. "This is Liz."

"Nice to meet you ladies. I'm Terri."

"Are you here for relaxation, Terri, or just to get away?"

"I'm actually doing some research on the area. I thought this would be the best way to get it."

"Great idea," Liz said. "I hope you get to spend some time out with one of those boys getting your research done."

The two women giggled as Terri frowned. She wasn't sure, but she thought she'd just been set up by the two older women who now seemed to be playing matchmaker with her. Yes, the men on the ranch were gorgeous from what she could tell. Each one had their own look about them, even the triplets. They were identical, but there were subtle differences between the two she'd seen. It made her wonder about the third, who wasn't there at the moment.

When she'd literally ran into Jason this morning, at first she'd thought he was Josh, but when she looked closer, she could definitely tell the difference. Joshua wasn't quite as broad across the shoulders as Jason. All the yummy hardness of both men made it difficult to decide which one was the cutest. She'd only observed the others from a distance except Jeff. The thought of that man made her frown as she glanced over the shoulder of the person in front of her to see him talking with Nina. His dark hair glinted in the lighting of the dining room, a blue-black color. Thick and straight to barely above his collar, she wanted to run her fingers through those silky looking strands.

Seconds later, he lifted his head and made immediate eye contact with her. A frown marred his features as his eyes narrowed.

Oh shit.

She dropped her gaze, moving behind the front person hoping he wouldn't confront her here in front of the other guests.

Cowboy boots appeared in her line of vision. *Damn it!*

"What the hell are you doin' here?"

"Excuse me?" she asked, lifting her head to stare into the stormy gray eyes of Jeff Young.

"You heard me. What are you doin' here on my family's ranch?"

Nina appeared at his side. "Jeff this is one of our guests. What's the problem?"

"She needs to leave."

"I'm not leaving. I'm a paid guest."

"Guest my ass. She's a damned spy," he snarled, his lips curling back in a ferocious look. He kind of reminded her of a pit bull with a bone protecting it from intruders.

Nina stepped between them and got in her son's face. "Enough, Jeff. Terri is a guest on our property no matter her reason for being here."

"I'm sure she'll report back to the developers on everything we do so they can undermine us or somethin'."

"Jeffery. I'll have no more talk like this. Go back to your seat."

"But, Ma…"

"But nothin'. Go on. We'll talk about this later."

His gaze snapped fire at her as he glared again before turning on his boots heels to head back to the table.

"I'm sorry, Terri."

"It's fine, Nina. Nothing to be sorry for. He doesn't like me at all."

"He sure does react to you rather oddly." Nina stared for a moment. "I'm sorry. Get your breakfast and I'll handle my eldest son at least until the meal is over. After that, I'm not sure what he'll do. He does have a temper."

"I can handle him."

Nina cocked her head. "You know. I think you can." She patted Terri on the shoulder before she returned to the family table.

"Wow. Interesting," Liz said, as they finally got to the serving table and grabbed their plates.

Terri smiled. She really didn't need the two older ladies getting in her business or being in the middle of what might become a knock down drag out with the eldest son of Thunder Ridge Guest Ranch.

* * * *

Jeff got his breakfast, all the while keeping a keen eye on the intruder. The spy. He knew she had to be up to no good if she decided to become a guest on his ranch. Something was up. He just knew it. He'd have to keep a close eye on her to make sure she didn't get information she could use against them with the land developers. *Damn it! I certainly don't need her snooping around right now.*

He returned to his place at the table with his and Ben's plate. "Here you go, buddy."

"What was that all about, Jeff?" Jeremiah asked, taking his chair.

"Nothin'."

"It didn't look like nothin' to me. You were all up in the woman's face."

"I said, it's nothin'."

"Fine, but as the financial planner of this ranch, if there somethin' goin' on that affects the financial stability, I need to know about it."

"You keep your nose in the books and leave the ranchin' to me."

"Kiss my ass, brother. Remember who controls the paychecks around here."

"Fuck you."

"What's with you lately?" Jackson asked, lifting the fork to his mouth. "You need a woman or somethin'?"

"The last fuckin' thing I need is a woman."

"Watch your mouth," Nina snapped. "We have guests present."

"Sorry, Ma."

"You shouldn't be cussin' around Ben anyway. He hears enough from you when you're out with the cattle, I'm sure."

"I think he needs to get laid," Jackson added with a grin. "It usually helps my mood."

"Your answer to everything is being between a woman's thighs."

"Why the heck not?" Jackson winked. "Sounds like a perfect place to me."

"Why were you in her face, Jeff?" Jason jumped in the middle of the conversation.

"What the hell do you care, Jason?"

Jason took a drink of his coffee. "I walked her to breakfast. She seems like a nice girl to me. Kinda pretty too."

"Just say away from her. She's trouble."

"What kinda trouble?" James asked, as Jeff finished his breakfast.

"Ma won't let me discuss it here. Let's just say, she needs to be off our property immediately."

"She's a paid guest, Jeff. I won't have you kickin' guests off the ranch. We need them to keep this place runnin'. She's paid up for two weeks."

"Two weeks?" Jeff growled. "What is she gonna do here for two weeks?"

"I didn't ask her when she paid up. What doesn't it matter anyway?"

"Just keep her away from me."

"You're the foreman on this ranch, Jeff," James said. "Your job is to keep everything runnin' smoothly. You'll be bound to run into her sometimes. We can't keep you two completely apart."

Jeff rolled his eyes. *Ah hell! This is gonna be the most miserable two weeks of my life if I have to constantly be nice to her.*

He glanced down at the end of the room to see Terri look his way. She was kind of pretty in a nerdy sort of way with her glasses, her hair back in a ponytail and those jeans. He frowned. At least she seemed to have gotten some jeans that didn't look like they just came off the rack at the western wear store or might leave a blue streak should she fall down snow skiing. The thought brought a smile to his lips. Imagining her with her butt in the middle of a snow bank while her new jeans bled into the snow almost made him laugh.

Skiing was one of his favorite pastimes and he hadn't had a chance to go in forever or at least since Ben had been born. Maybe this winter he'd be able to convince his mom to watch Ben and he could take off for a weekend by himself.

He shook his head. Getting involved with a guest was against the rules anyway you sliced it, even if he wanted to. Terri was trouble with a capital T.

A heavy sigh left his lips. He had work to do. "You stay with Grandma, Ben. I'm headed to the barn, Ma. I need to inventory the feed and see what we need to order."

"Go head, Jeff." She grabbed Ben in a big hug and set him on her hip. "We got this covered, right, Ben?"

"Yep. You go on, Daddy."

Jeff rolled his eyes and laughed. His kid was growing up way too fast.

He walked outside glancing around for what he wasn't sure. *Liar. You're lookin' for Terri.* He didn't want to care about what she might be doing right now, but he did. After he told himself he needed to keep an eye out for her to make sure she wasn't doing something she shouldn't, he felt like kicking his own ass for being stupid.

Why he kept her real purpose for being in Bandera a secret from his family, he wasn't sure. Maybe he wanted to give her the benefit of the doubt. *Why? I know she works for the developers. She told me she did.* "She's up to no good. I know she is."

He headed to the barn with a sharp stomp to his step. His anger bubbled inside him making him all the more pissy as he grabbed the clipboard from the doorway on his way inside. *Damn meddling woman. She needs to go, but how do I get her to leave?*

"Maybe if I make her time here miserable, she'll leave on her own?"

"Jeff?" Joey called coming into the barn.

"In the back, Joe."

"I've got a horse I want to go look at over at the Marshall place."

"So? Why are you tellin' me?"

"So you can watch the horses."

"Where is Jacob or Jonathan?"

"Hell if I know. It's not my job to keep track of the rest of the bunch. I'm just tellin' you where I'm going so you can watch them. There's a group out now with Jackson on the trail. They just left and won't be back for an hour."

"Great. Just great. I have my own work to do and now I have to do yours?"

Joey grinned. "You can clean some tack while I'm gone."

"Fuck you, Joe. Cleanin' the tack is your damned job."

"Yeah and so is breakin' the horses so they don't throw the guests, but I don't see you helpin' with that either, big man."

"I ain't got time to do everyone's fuckin' job along with my own."

"You wanted the foreman job, buddy. You got it." Joey waved and headed off toward where the cars were parked. "I'll be back in a couple of hours."

"The Marshall property is five goddamn minutes from here."

"Yes it is, but I still need to check the stock. See ya!"

"Fuckin' son of a bitch." He threw the clipboard across the barn.

He headed for the tack room so he could keep an eye on the horses in the corral. Why, he wasn't sure. It wasn't like they were going anywhere, but a guest might have questions so he needed to be there. He could clean tack. *Fuck that!*

A soft voice came from the doorway. "Jeff?"

Great. Terri. "What do you want?" he asked with a snarl. He wasn't about to make it easy on her.

She twisted the end of her T-shirt between her fingers. He obviously made her a little nervous. "I'm sorry things have gotten off on the wrong foot between us."

"We aren't on any damned foot, lady. You're here under false pretenses and I don't like it."

"I'm not here to spy. I need to ask questions and the best people to ask are the locals. I figured cowboys knew the lay of the land the best."

"Why us?"

"Because your land is adjacent to the land the developers purchased for their housing development. Your land is very similar to the land over there."

"I'm not helpin' you."

"Fine. I'll ask one of your brothers. Two of the triplets have been nice enough to me. I'm sure I can get one of them to talk."

"Leave my brothers out of this. This is between you and me."

"There's nothing between you and me, Mr. Young. You're a self-centered bully who thinks he can intimidate me because I'm a woman. Well forget it. You won't drive me away from doing my job. It's all I'm trying to do and—"

Jeff stepped closer, wrapped his hand around the back of her head, and slammed his mouth against hers.

She pulled back. "What the hell?"

He did it again, but this time her lips softened under his, molding themselves to the curve of his mouth. His hand tangled in her ponytail, pulling her head back slightly so he could deepen the kiss. With the tip of his tongue tracing the seam of her lips, he asked for her to open for him. Her lips parted on a moan. He pulled her hair harder. Her moan deepened into a low growl in her throat. Their tongues danced, tangling together from her mouth to his and back. His hand left her hair to trace the curve of her neck.

Thinking beyond how her mouth felt under his left his brain in a fog.

Her hands fisted in his shirt, pulling him closer still.

The clink of a horses bridle brought him out of the mist with a startled step back. "I'm sorry. I…"

"You what?"

"I shouldn't have lost control. You're a guest."

"So?"

"We don't mess with guests."

"Well apparently some of you do if your brother married a woman who was a guest here at one time."

"That's different."

"Different how? You're the one who kissed me."

"Just go back to your cottage and leave me the hell alone, would you please?"

She fisted her hands on her hips. "No. I need your expertise to answer some questions."

"I'm not telling you anythin'."

"We can go round and round about this for days, Jeff. If you help me, I'll be gone sooner."

"Sooner?"

She nodded as she swept her hair back and fixed her ponytail where he'd almost pulled it out of its confinement. "Yes. I won't stay the entire two weeks if I get the information I need."

Maybe helping her would help him. Surely she didn't need personal information about the ranch, just general stuff. "What kind of information do you need?"

"How many cattle do you run?" she asked, pulling out a pen and small pad of paper from her pocket.

"I can't tell you that."

Air rush from between her lips in a heavy sigh as she tipped her head back on her shoulders. "What are the native trees to the area?"

"Texas Junipers and several other types of brush. I can't name them all, but you could get samples I guess."

"Rock types?"

He told her what he knew.

"Do you have to supplement your cattle with feed often?" she asked, biting her lip.

Damn, she was turning him inside out with her innocent gesture. "During dry summers, yes."

"How did the rainfall go this year in comparison to years previously?"

Their conversation went on this way for over an hour while he sat with her in the tack room. The guests who'd been out with one of his brothers on a run had come and gone, but still she asked more questions than he could give her answers for and some he wasn't willing to. If it meant she'd go away, then so be it. He could get on with his life if she wasn't nearby.

Damn. Why did I kiss her?

He shook his head as he remembered his dream from the night before. After she'd given him a blowjob, he'd fucked her senseless in his bed. Now she stood in front of him with her lips still red and swollen from his kiss. A kiss he shouldn't have given her on a good day, much less how they'd started off.

"Hello?"

"Sorry. My mind wandered. What did you ask?"

"How many guests do you all have in a good year?"

"I'm not tellin' you that either." He stood up from his spot on the edge of the metal desk. "Look. You should have all the information you need. You can go now."

"No, I need to ride out to the property line between your ranch and the development so I can see what types of rocks and plant life are there. Will you take me?" she asked, chewing her lips again.

"You can't be serious."

"Of course I am. George got the measurements he needed for the survey, but I need a more up close look at the landscape."

"No, I meant you can't be serious about me taking you out there." He folded his arms over his chest. "Darlin', I already helped you more than I should with what you are tryin' to do to this countryside."

"Darlin'?"

"Never mind. We're done here."

"Please, Jeff?" She placed her hand on his arm. He didn't like the warmth spreading up the appendage. Usually that kind of reaction meant trouble, especially when she stepped close enough he could smell her shampoo. Vanilla. Damn, he loved the smell of vanilla. "It won't take long."

"Fine. When Joey gets back from…"

A honk sounded outside as Joey pulled up the ranch truck in front of the tack barn.

"I take it that's Joey?"

"Sorry. I hadn't realized you didn't already know all of my brothers."

Joey stepped out of the truck and slammed the door. "Howdy, ma'am."

"Hi."

"Joey, this is Terri. Terri Kennedy, this is the youngest of the group, Joey."

"Nice to meet you, ma'am." He tipped his hat.

"You, too." She nodded to the trailer. "What do you have in there?"

"A new mare for the brood. Want to take a look?"

"Sure. I love horses."

"She's a filly so I need to train her, but she's a beauty. Black as the midnight sky with a pretty blaze on her nose." Joey popped open the trailer's back door and slid inside to unhook the horse's lead rope. "Such a pretty girl." The filly's ears flicked back and forth to the sound of his voice. There was a good reason Joey took care of the animals. He had a way with the ladies especially.

"Oh my! She's beautiful."

"She'll make some pretty colts, I bet," Joey said, stroking her as he backed her out of the trailer. "Easy now." The horse's withers shook as she stepped out onto the solid ground.

"You did good, Joe." His compliment earned him a scowl. Surely he hadn't been so hard on his brothers lately they all hated him.

"Thanks, Jeff." Joey glanced between him and Terri with a raised eyebrow. "I'm gonna take her into the barn. Since I'm back, you can go about doin' whatever you needed to do earlier, Jeff."

"Actually, I'm goin' to take Terri out to one of the pastures. She needs to check some things out over there."

"Really?" she asked, surprise written all over her face.

"Yeah."

"Well, the group is back, aren't they?"

"Yeah."

"You can take any of the horses then."

"I'll get her set up."

"See you two later." Joey led the new filly toward the barn.

"How much ridin' have you done?"

"Some, but not recently. I mean I can stay on one and make them go where I want them to. I don't consider myself an expert by any means."

"Most of our horses are very tame. We have a lot of beginner riders but I don't want to give you one who won't do anything either."

"Mediocre then?"

He chuckled, startling himself and Terri. It had been a long damn time since anyone made him smile, much less laugh.

"You have a nice laugh."

A sobering thought ripped across his mind. He didn't have anything to be happy about. His life sucked right now. Unfortunately, he didn't see it getting better anytime soon.

"I didn't mean to upset you."

"You didn't. I have a lot on my mind is all." He headed back into the tack room to grab his saddle while she followed on his heels. Why in the hell had he agreed to take her out to the property line anyway? The last thing he needed was to encourage her into thinking he might be okay with this damned crap with the developers when he wasn't. "Let's get this over with."

"I'm sure I could get one of your brothers to take me, if you would rather not."

"I'll do it. Besides, I want to keep an eye on you."

"I'm not trying to do anything illegal, Jeff. I need to see a few things."

"We've had this discussion, Terri. I don't want you on our property. The sooner you leave the better for everyone, especially me."

"Why especially you?"

"I don't like you."

She stepped forward and ran her fingernail down his chest. "Your problem is I think you like me a little too much."

With her fingers in his fist, he snapped, "No, I don't."

"Then why'd you kiss me?" she asked, glancing up through her lashes with those incredibly green eyes.

"Hell if I know, but it won't happen again." He started to push past her, but she stopped him dead in his tracks with her words.

"What if I want it to?"

A lump formed in his throat and he swallowed hard to push his words past it. "Well, it won't. I don't need a woman in my life. I don't need you."

"Not even for a little bit of quick fun?"

His cock hardened behind the fly of his pants at the sultry sound of her whispered words. His dream came back to haunt him in the flesh as she stood there promising him sweet release if he'd only give into the desires blazing between them. "What'd you have in mind?"

"You seem like you could use a good romp in the hay. I'm just thinking we could help each other out a little. It's been a bit for me and from the conversations around the ranch, it sounds like it has for you too."

"Let's get this ride over with."

"And then we'll talk more?"

"Maybe."

She smiled with a sexy little tip of her lips that drove desire straight to his balls. *I'm so fuckin' screwed.*

Chapter Four

They rode along with the sun beating down on their shoulders. Sweat trickled down her back between her shoulder blades. She wiped at the moisture on her forehead wishing she would have thought to bring water.

Jeff reached into his saddle bag and brought out a water bottle. He handed it over as she sighed in relief.

"Thank you."

"You're welcome, city girl."

"I'm not a city girl."

"Could have fooled me. Who rides out here without bringin' water?"

"I didn't think…"

"Yeah, I know. Good thing I did, huh?"

"Ass-wipe," she grumbled under her breath.

"What did you say?" he asked with a grin.

"Nothing." She really did like his smile even though right at the moment she'd like to wipe it off his lips with her fist or a kiss. She wasn't sure which one and it bothered her.

How far it would be until they reached the property line, she wasn't sure.

Several types of plant life made it into jotted notes of her book while the rode along. Rocks and animal life got noted too. The more information she had, the better her report to the developers would be. This job meant a lot of money to her fledgling company so she had to do her best.

"What are they plannin' on doin'?"

"Dividing up the property into five acres parcels, building a few houses on them to get started and then selling off the plots so people can build their own."

"Wonderful. Just fuckin' wonderful," he snapped.

She reached over to lay her hand on his arm. For some reason his misery at the prospects bothered her. "I'm sorry, Jeff. I know you don't want to be a part of this, but its progress. You have to look at it in the sense where it's going to be good for the community to have the additional population here. It will help the local stores, restaurants, bars, and your family's ranch."

"How in the hell will it help us?"

"Think of it this way. People will come to visit family and friends who live in the new development. If they don't have a place to stay, they'll stay at Thunder Ridge. You have a great set up! You can teach them about cowboying and how to live life with the cattle as part of your life verses the citified people coming out here to mess up the land."

"Maybe."

"It's true."

"I have to have somethin' to leave my son when he's grown." He shook his head, glancing at her even though she couldn't see those arresting gray eyes beneath his sunglasses. "We won't sell off any of our property to them. They have to know that."

"You'll have the land to give Ben. The developers aren't looking for more at the moment." The horse shifted under her as she grabbed the pommel in a death grip. It really had been a long time since she'd been on a horse, but it came back like riding a bike.

"Right now, they ain't, but what if they do in five years or even ten?"

"If you aren't selling, what difference does it make which way they expand?"

"More and more people tearing up the roads, using up the land, dammin' up the water for their own use. All of those things take away from what we've built here."

"You can't keep living in the past, Jeff."

"I don't want things to change."

"Change is good."

"Not always."

She continued to mull over what he said. True, change wasn't always for the best, but in this case it had to be. Her life and her job depended on it being the right thing to do.

They came around a large boulder to see a barbed wire fence stretching far into the distance in both directions.

"This is the property line." He leaned over the pommel of his saddle, resting his forearms across the padded leather in a relaxed, totally cowboy state. "Do what you need to do."

She swung her leg over the back of the horse and dropped her booted feet into the loose gravel. She grabbed the binoculars from around her neck and scanned the area. Several birds flew out of a nearby bush into the afternoon sky. With a note in her book, she described the birds in as much details as she could. Their species might be important in the long run.

"I'll hold her while you look around," Jeff said, swinging down from his own horse. "There's a small spring over here to the right. I'll water them."

"Okay." She sighed as she took her pen and paper in her hand to make some notes. After several minutes, she glanced off to the right where she heard the spring tinkling down over the rocks. Instead of making the notes she needed to make and the drawings of the area, she found herself wandering to where Jeff said he was going. *Surely they had the same rocks and bushes over there, right?*

"Jeff?"

"Over here." She followed his voice until she saw him crouched down near a pool.

"How pretty."

"It's one of the natural springs we have running through our property. This one has a great little swimmin' area right here." He pointed to the two boulders on the other side with a sweep of his hand. "It's not terribly deep but you can swim in it. I bet it would feel good right now."

"Can we put our feet in?"

"Sure."

She giggled as she quickly stripped off her boots and socks before she rolled up her pant legs. The water felt cold on her feet when she dipped them in, but after the heat of the day during their ride, it felt like heaven. "Lordy, that's great!"

Jeff took the rock next to her and dipped his feet in too. "We used to come up here swimmin' when we were kids much to my mother's disappointment. Came home wet all the time."

"I can totally see you and your brothers getting into trouble with your mom. She's a strong lady."

"Yes, she is. She's the glue holdin' this whole ranch together. God forbid somethin' happen to her, none of us would know what to do."

They sat in silence for several minutes while she contemplated the man near her. He really didn't seem so grouchy while he sat with her dipping their feet in the cool water. She wondered more about him. How had he grown up? He seemed like such a strong man, but around Ben he buckled under to be the dad the boy needed in his life. He ran the ranch with an iron fist, but seeing how he handled his younger brothers, she thought he needed to let up on them some.

"What are you thinkin' about?"

"You."

"Me? Why me?"

"I'm wondering about you is all. You've had it pretty rough from what I've heard."

"Not really. I've had a great life livin' out here on the place I grew up. I love runnin' the ranch, doin' the chores, workin' with the animals. You know, ranch stuff."

"I can see that."

"What do you do when you aren't out in a place like this? You seem like a city girl to me."

"I live in Houston. I have my own architecture firm."

"Definitely a city girl." He laughed when she frowned.

"I'm not either."

"What do you call those clothes you were wearin' yesterday with your fancy boots and designer jeans?"

"All right. I don't have worn boots like yours or ripped jeans, but I'm not a city girl like New York or Los Angeles. Houston isn't the city."

"Sure it is."

"No, it's not." She cupped her hand in the water before she tossed the small trickle onto him.

"Hey!" He threw some back at her.

Within minutes, she stood halfway in the middle of the pond to her waist, soaking wet while they laughed like children as they splashed each other. Jeff stood at the edge with the water to his calves, but his jeans and T-shirt were soaked too. She bit her lip while she stared at the material clinging to his chest. The muscles rippled beneath the material when he moved. *Damn, he's got a magnificent chest and abs.*

He quickly flung off his hat and rushed into the water as she squealed and tried to get away. "No! Wait," she shouted right before he pushed her under. She came up sputtering with her hair partially in her face. "You've done it now, cowboy."

"Come after me, babe! You don't have what it takes."

"Oh no?" She rushed him, jumping full into his chest and taking them both down into the water. They broke the surface together laughing while she clung to his shoulders. A moment later, she realized how close their mouths were as she looked up into his gray eyes that turned to molten silver with lust.

His cock hard between their straining bodies kicked up her desire to raging. She could feel every inch of him against her stomach. Water clung to his lashes, making them looked like diamonds in the sunlight. The man was beautiful.

Silence stretched between them. She wasn't sure what to do. She wanted to feel his mouth against her again, feel the heat raging between them. "Kiss me."

"I shouldn't."

"But you want to."

"Yeah, I do."

"Then do it." She sucked in a ragged breath, blowing it out on a sigh. "Afraid?"

He dragged her closer still. "I'm not afraid of you."

The hard plains of his chest brushed against her peaked nipples. Her whole body ached from wanting to be closer, needing to be closer. "You're afraid of what you want to do to me. You think because we're supposed to be enemies, you shouldn't want to fuck me."

"I don't want to fuck you."

She tossed back her hair and laughed. "Have you got a salami in your pocket then?"

"Fine," he growled. "I want to fuck you until the sun drops in the western sky. I want to bury myself in your sweet heat and let you scald me until this need for you burns out like a blue flame."

"Then do it cowboy. Right here, right now."

He picked her up by the waist and she wrapped her legs around his middle. She wanted this, needed this more than her next breath. Ever since she'd first run into this tortured, lonely man, she'd wanted to hold him, comfort him and fuck him into tomorrow.

The fine gravel lining the edges of the pond bit into her back when he laid her down. His fingers made quick work of the front of her shirt, parting it to reveal her water soaked bra to his gaze. "Beautiful."

He took her nipple into his mouth, sucking it through the sheer fabric of her bra. Her whole body hummed as he bit the flesh. "Ah, God." Within seconds, he had her bra open and her breasts revealed to his scorching gaze.

The warmth of the sun quickly dried the water on her skin as he peeled open her jeans. The wet fabric clung to her, making it difficult for him to work his hand into the parted material. A brush of his fingers over her throbbing nub shot her straight into mega arousal. "Please, Jeff."

"You're so slick."

"I want you inside me." He worked his fingers into her grasping pussy while his thumb worked her clit.

"I want you to come for me."

"Now? But…"

"You can do it. I feel your body vibrating around my fingers."

He stroked her clit quickly. Her body shot straight through the buildup to orgasm in seconds flat. Her scream of his name bounced off the rocks around them, drifting off on the wind as she slowly came back down, blinking in surprise at the intensity of her orgasm.

"You're beautiful when you come."

"Thanks." She frowned. "I think."

"Jeff?" someone shouted from their left.

"Oh hell!" Terri quickly scrambled out from under him, trying desperately to right her clothing.

"Stay where you are, Jackson."

"I ain't movin'. I'll stay right here and enjoy the scenery."

The sound came from the rocks not very far away. "He can't see me, can he?" she asked, putting the finishing touches on her clothing. *Shit. His brother probably heard me scream out my orgasm. How embarrassing.*

"I'm not sure where he's sittin', but I doubt he missed your scream."

"Thanks, Jeff."

"You're welcome, darlin'."

He grinned like a Cheshire cat, the jerk. At least his brother didn't catch them in the middle of having sex. *He probably would have if he'd waited a few more minutes to make his presence known.*

"What are you doin' out here, Jackson?"

"Lookin' for you. Joey said you were comin' out here to the property line. I came to tell you the feed store brought the load."

"You couldn't have waited until I got back?"

"You're always bitchin' when we don't tell you the load is here."

Jeff didn't respond to that.

"Took a swim, did ya?"

"Give the lady some privacy, will ya?"

"I ain't lookin'. I heard the splashin' from a mile away."

Which means he heard me scream. Just fucking great.

"Jackson, you can come down now."

"Thank you, ma'am." He appeared moments later around the crop of rocks not a hundred yards away. "I don't think we've met," he said, holding out his hand. "Jackson, ma'am. I'm the second eldest behind Jeff."

She blushed to the roots of her hair as his laughing gaze trailed down her body. "Terri Kennedy. It's nice to meet you."

"Enjoy your swim?"

"Yes, actually. It was very refreshing."

"Sounded like it."

The small smirk on Jackson's face made her want to slap it right off his lips. "I believe we're done here, right Jeff?"

"Yeah. We were about to head back anyway. You can go on home, Jackson."

Jackson swung up onto the back of his horse and tipped his hat as he kicked the gelding into a canter, riding off into the brush.

"I'm so embarrassed."

"Don't be."

"Why the hell not? He probably heard me scream your name as I came all over your fingers!"

"True, but it ain't like he hasn't heard it before," Jeff replied, earning himself her ire.

"You bring a lot of women out here and fuck their brains out?"

"I didn't fuck your brains out, Terri. If you remember correctly, I didn't get to come…yet."

"So sorry. Should I take care of it for you before we head back?" Her sarcasm seemed lost on him.

"Not necessary right at the moment, darlin', but I wouldn't mind visitin' you later in your cabin."

"I thought there was some kind of rule about you guys and the guests?"

"Who told you?"

She shrugged as she examined her fingernails on her left hand. "You told me in the tack room, remember? You do have a little gaggle of geese who love to follow you around with their gaze just like the rest of your brothers."

He scuffed his boot in the dirt. "We do have the rule."

"Well I guess you already broke it since you fingered me to orgasm a few minutes ago." She picked at her wet clothes hoping they didn't chafe her thighs on the ride back to the ranch. "I guess you could come by my cabin after supper." The thought sent a thrill through her belly. The thought of actually making love with this man brought another rush of heat to her cheeks. Yeah, she'd gotten off with a pretty terrific orgasm, but he hadn't. Riding back to the ranch with a hard-on probably wouldn't be the most comfortable thing to do. Oh well, it couldn't be helped. He really did need to get back if Jackson's conversation meant anything.

"Listen, Terri. Maybe this isn't such good idea."

"What?"

"Us."

"I didn't think there really was an us, but why not?"

"Well there is sort of. I just think with our differences of opinion on the land development, your involvement in it, and how I feel about it, we shouldn't be doin' anythin' together."

"We're fucking, Jeff. Nothing more. It's a little release from the pressures of everyday life. Don't read more into it than there is."

"I'm not. I don't need a woman in my life. In fact, it's the last damned thing I need."

"Maybe if you did have a woman, you wouldn't be to fucking up tight!"

"Uptight? I'm not uptight!"

"Bullshit! You're wound so damned tight, I'm surprised your dick even works!" She climbed back into the saddle as she watched the magnificent butt of the man next to her, do the same thing.

"I'll show you how well my dick works, baby. Just spread them thighs, this dick will make your pussy weep."

"Only because I haven't had any dick in two years." She turned her horse back toward the house. "Any dick would do."

"You want dick, honey, you come lookin' for me. You'll stay away from my brothers."

"I'll fuck whomever I want."

"No, you will not!"

His face looked thunderous so she backed off. She didn't know the exact details of his past relationships, but obviously there was something there she didn't want to go into. It wasn't like she wanted any of his brothers anyway. She wanted him. Pain in the ass and all.

Chapter Five

The supper bell clanged as Jeff stood in the doorway of the barn watching the guests wander toward the main lodge. Should he join the family for supper or not? He really wasn't sure. If he did, would it give Terri the impression he would join her afterward? Maybe. Should he? He didn't know. He wanted to. God, did he want to.

Everything about her turned him inside out. He wanted to see her blonde curls spread out over the pillow as he pounded into her hot flesh or tickling his abdomen while she sucked his cock until he squirted cum down her throat.

He'd never wanted a woman so badly before. The thought drove him nuts.

"Are you going in?" Joey asked, coming from the stable to the left of the barn.

"Yeah, I'll be there in a second. I need to check on something."

Joey shrugged and walked toward the house. "Hey, Ms. Terri." He waved as he caught Terri walking up the concrete path toward the house.

Jeff watched from the barn doors while Joey caught up with her and walked her into supper. Jealousy surged through him, catching him unaware. Jealousy? Why should he be jealous? He didn't care a whit about her. Well, maybe a little, but he couldn't get caught up in her at all.

Hurting her didn't fit with his plans either. He didn't want to hurt her. He hoped she wasn't thinking anything between them could go on and turn into anything permanent. He didn't do permanent. Not anymore.

Ben came running from the swing set they'd put up for him in the side garden. "Come on, Daddy. It's supper time."

"I'm comin', son."

Jeff followed Ben's little body to the house. Smiling, he ran up behind him, grabbed him and swung him up on his shoulders, much to the gleeful squeals of his son.

When they walked inside the building, he caught Terri's gaze from her spot to his right. She sat with a group of women chattering away, but she remained silent as she watched him set Ben down. *Damn, she's pretty.* She didn't wear a lot of makeup. Her clean complexion glowed with healthy vibrance as her gorgeous green eyes sparkled with something he wasn't sure he wanted to name. He tipped his hat, catching her little half smile when he walked by her table.

The ladies twittered around her, but he kept walking. He didn't want anyone to get the idea there was anything going on between them. *Jackson better keep his big mouth shut.*

As he approached the family table and his assigned chair, the family got quiet. "What?"

"How did the ride go?" his mother asked, tilting her head to the side as she grinned.

"What ride?"

"Jackson went out to find you and Terri, right?"

He glared at his brother who just laughed. "Yeah, he did. The ride went fine. I showed her where the property lines are so she could get some samples and take some notes. The quicker she's gone, the better for all of us."

"Better for you?"

"Yes. I don't want her here."

"It didn't sound that way to me," Jackson said with a laugh.

"Shut up."

"She's really not causing any harm, Jeff. I'd rather she be here so we can keep an eye on what she's doing, which by the way, you haven't explained to the rest of us."

"I'll handle her, Ma."

"I think you already did," Jackson added.

"I told you to shut the fuck up."

"Jeffery!"

"Sorry, but he's crossin' the line."

"You'll not talk like that at the dinner table with the guests here. I've discussed this with you before."

"I said I'm sorry."

"Fine." She glanced at Jackson. "Apparently you have a secret between you and your brother. I would appreciate it if you would keep it to yourself. There is no need to discuss it in front of family or guests."

"Sorry, Ma."

"You should be. Whatever is part of Jeffery's private life is private. Keep it that way."

"Yes, ma'am," Jackson replied although Jeff could see the twinkle of mischief in his eyes. It wasn't over by a long shot.

Once supper was over, he needed to get someone to watch Ben for a few hours and needed to figure out a way to be able to get into Terri's cabin without being seen. Not like he planned to stay the night or anything, but he couldn't leave his son alone in their home without someone to keep an eye on him. He debated on whether to ask Jackson since he already knew about Jeff and Terri's rendezvous by the pond, but he also debated on whether to ask his mother. What would she think? *She'd be jumping my shit for fuckin' a guest.* "Of course, she was all over gettin' Joel and Mesa together."

The guests cleared the dining room leaving the family to finish up their own supper.

"Mom, can you watch Ben for a couple of hours?"

"Of course, Jeff. Do you have plans?"

"Yeah. I need to go into town for a bit."

"I know it's been a long time since you've been around a female, son." She patted his hand. "I'll watch Ben."

Jeff glanced at the ceiling as he sighed. *Great. Mom thinks I'm headed out to find a woman.* "Thanks, Mom."

She winked.

I obviously didn't fool her one bit.

Jeff cleared his and Ben's plates before he hustled his son back outside with the intention of getting him home and in bed before his mother came over to watch him. He hoped his mom didn't know who he planned to fuck tonight, but at this moment, he didn't care.

Remember when you gave Joel shit for fuckin' Mesa?

He really should apologize to his brother when the two of them got back from their honeymoon. He did come down pretty hard on Joel for sleeping with a guest when here he was about to do the same thing and enjoy every damned minute of it if this afternoon had been any indicator. Terri was hotter than a firecracker on the Fourth of July. She's been spectacular when she'd come apart in his arms by the pond. He'd never seen a woman look so beautiful when she came. He hoped to fuck her face to face so he could see it again.

Hell, who was he kidding? He wanted her any way he could get her. In her hot pussy, up her delicious looking ass, in her mouth. He didn't care.

"Daddy?"

"Yes, Ben," he replied as they walked through the front door of their cabin.

"How come Mommy doesn't come over anymore?"

He took Ben's hand and headed into the bathroom to get his bath ready. "I don't know, son. I guess she's busy."

"I want to stay at her house."

Jeff got worried. Ben never said he wanted to stay at Misha's. Whenever he did go over there, by the time she brought him back, he was difficult to deal with for a few days afterward. Sometimes, it was like there wasn't any discipline at her house, which he figured was the case. "Why?"

Ben took off his clothes and climbed into the warm water Jeff had run into the tub. "She lets me eat chocolate ice cream and watch Dora."

"You do those things here too."

"How come Mommy doesn't love me?" Ben asked, playing with his truck absently in the bubbles.

"I'm sure she does in her own way, Ben."

"She never says it like you do. You always say you love me."

"Because I do, Ben. I love you very much."

"I love you too, Daddy."

The conversation drifted off into other topics, like his horse, when Grandma was coming over and did he really have to go to bed. The normal things they talked about almost every night.

"Will you read me a story, Daddy?"

"Of course, son. We're still reading the Tommy the Train book, right?"

"Yes," Ben answered, climbing into the bed.

Jeff tucked the covers around his shoulders. The book they'd be reading sat on the nightstand next to the bed. Jeff read five pages before he glanced at his son to find him sound asleep. He put the book back on the stand, turned off the light and closed the door as he walked out.

He found his mother on the couch with her knitting.

"I didn't hear you come in."

"I know. You were tucking Ben in. I heard you reading."

"Thanks for coming over, Mom."

"You're welcome, honey. I know you need some time out. You need adult company. It's normal for a man your age."

"It's not a big deal."

"Sure it is. I understand men's needs. Just remember, we women have them too. Take your time tonight. No hurry to be home. I'll stay until the morning if you want."

"Not necessary. I'll only be gone a couple of hours."

"Whatever you want, Jeff."

He grabbed his keys off the hook next to the door where he always kept them, put on his cowboy hat and opened the door.

"Tell Terri hello for me."

"Mom?"

"Yes, dear."

He shook his head. He knew better than to question how his mother knew things. "Never mind. Thanks."

"You're welcome." She blew him a kiss as he shut the door behind him.

Darkness surrounded him. Stars winked overhead. No moon tonight to light the way but he knew the land like the back of his hand. He hopped in his truck and drove the two minutes it took to get from his cabin back to the main lodge area. He wasn't sure which cabin Terri was even in so he hoped she waited for him on the porch.

He pulled down the driveway and stopped near the parking area for the guests. Terri sat in a rocking chair on the porch of her cabin, directly in front of where he parked. He took a deep breath, checked his wallet for condoms and then stepped out.

"Hey."

"Hi. I wasn't sure if you were going to show up or not."

"Why wouldn't I? The promise of great sex is a promise I don't want to pass up."

"Yeah, but I wasn't sure you'd have someone to watch Ben tonight or a hundred other reasons why you might have changed your mind." She tucked a piece of hair behind her ear as she rocked in the chair.

Her hair lay on her shoulders caressing them like a lover's hand. He wanted to run his fingers through the silky strands. Her green eyes sparkled behind her glasses when she raked her gaze down his frame. It set him on fire to see the lust in her eyes.

He held out his hand, waiting for her to take it into her grasp so he could pull her into his arms. The porch light on her cabin outlined them for anyone to see, but tonight, he didn't care. Let them talk.

"You look so pretty sitting there."

She took his hand and stood.

"Thank you. You look pretty handsome yourself you know."

"Shall we go inside?"

"Sure."

He opened her cabin door, tugging her along behind him. Being with Terri made him feel like a sixteen-year-old kid with his first fuck, and he wasn't sure why. Yes, she was a beautiful woman, but he almost felt like he might get caught by her parents or his. Hell, at thirty-four years old, he should be over this feeling by now. *It must be the anticipation.*

"I'm nervous."

"Why?" he asked.

"I'm not sure. It's not like we haven't been together before, but I guess not like this."

He raised her hand as he entwined their fingers. "We don't have to do this if you don't want to."

"But I do," she whispered.

He slid his right hand along her jawline and then into her hair. "You have beautiful hair. It's so soft."

"Thanks."

Her lips called to him to taste. He slowly drew her closer, watching as her lips parted in anticipation. The need to feel her mouth under his drove everything out of his mind.

"Can you see at all without these?"

"Close up, yes."

He took off her glasses and set them on the nightstand. "You have beautiful eyes."

"You talk too much, Jeff. Kiss me."

He slipped both hands along her jaw and into her hair, pulling her closer as his mouth brushed hers. The softness enveloped him. He needed to bring her closer still. The feel of her lips under his drove his desire higher and made his cock swell behind the fly of his jeans. The need to be inside her overwhelmed him. He'd never gotten this hard this fast with any other woman. Not even Misha and he thought he loved her.

Lust, old man. Just lust.

She took two fistfuls of his shirt and popped the snaps in one swift tug. The moment, she tore her mouth from his, she said,

"Damn, you have a nice chest. And look at those abs? A real six-pack."

Her lips did a little dance along his neck until she reached his ear. Her teeth nipped at his earlobe.

Damn, the woman took over like a Domme. He wondered if she might be into a little rough sex. Not like he would give up control, but he kind of liked her taking over their love making a little bit.

"Let me please you."

Her mouth trailed down his chest, biting at his nipples with her teeth, drawing on them with the tip of her tongue. His flesh erupted in a huge mass of goose bumps. She followed the line of hair down his chest, across his abdomen to the waistband of his jeans. Her tiny hands worked the belt buckle loose and drew the zipper down before she tugged his jeans and briefs down around his thighs. The moment she took him into her mouth, he almost exploded.

The feeling of her sucking on his cock, her mouth doing sensational things to him had him shaking so hard he could barely stand. "Terri, wait." He tried to pull her up but she refused to let go of his cock. She sucked harder, drawing his climax to the breaking point. He lost control and came deep in her throat in an explosion of cum he could barely handle. "Oh God!" She licked and sucked until he felt drained. "You didn't have to do that."

She glanced up through her lashes. "I know, but I wanted to. You took my anxiety level down a notch earlier by the pond. I figured it would help keep the second time from being a five minute race to see who came first."

"Smart woman."

She smiled before she enveloped him in her warm mouth again.

"Easy lady. You're gonna be the death of me."

A giggle escaped her mouth as he drew her up to her feet and kissed her. The taste of his cum on her lips felt almost weird, but gave him a sense of completeness with her. She took care of him in a way no woman had done before. "Your turn, darlin'."

He drew her tank top over her head, leaving her completely bare from the waist up. "You are so beautiful, you take my breath away."

"You're just saying that."

"No. It's true."

"I'm sure you've been with woman far prettier than I am."

"Maybe so, but they didn't have the inner beauty you have. The love of life. The light shining from your soul. You're a truly beautiful woman."

"Thank you, but you don't have to say that to get laid. You're already gonna get laid."

He grinned and raised an eyebrow. "Good, because I can't wait to be inside you."

With a slight push, she sprawled out on the bed in a heap of glorious hair and lusty green eyes. He unsnapped her jeans and drew them off her hips. Her painted toes peeked out of the hem of her jeans in all their pink glory. *Such a girlie girl. She'd never fit on the ranch in any capacity with her city girl ways, pink toenails and designer jeans.*

He got her jeans and underpants off in one fell swoop, and then divested himself of the rest of his clothing so he could concentrate on pleasuring her. She never moved from her spot on the bed.

Her glistening pussy called to him to taste, to explore. He swiped one finger over her pussy, across her clit and skimmed her puffy little lips hiding the rest of her from his gaze.

"Touch me more."

"I'm going to. I'm gonna make you cream for me."

"Like earlier?"

"Even more so."

He crouched on the floor between her legs and pulled her so her pussy was right on the edge of the bed. One swipe of his tongue on her clit had her moaning her need. Good. He wanted her to come apart under his mouth. He needed her to lose control with him. It had been too long since he'd had a woman in his arms.

She groaned softly, her head swinging back and forth on the comforter. Both her fists grasped the bedding beneath her as he worked his mouth on her pussy. He licked, sucked, fingered and sucked more on the tasty flesh beneath his mouth. With two fingers deep inside her, he could feel her coming unraveled. Her cries of ecstasy sounded raw and emotional to his ears, like it had been a very long time since she'd had a climax so strong. He couldn't wait to be inside her when she came apart again. He grabbed his pants, fished out a condom and rolled it on his aching flesh.

The high bed frame put her in perfect line with his cock when he stood and eased his cock inside her hot pussy. "You're incredible."

"Fuck me, Jeff. Hard. Give it to me hard. Please. God, I need you."

The sensation in his balls made him ache to slam into her with enough force to scoot her across the bed. "I might hurt you."

"You can't hurt me. I need it. Harder, please."

He slammed his groin against hers in a desperate attempt to get closer. He needed to be closer. Pelvis to groin, cock to pussy, eating her up with everything inside him. They rocked the bedframe as he fucked her with every fiber of his being until he got so close to coming he thought he would combust into a ball of flames. "Come with me, Terri."

"Rub my clit. I need the friction to come again."

He shook his head not only to clear his thoughts, but to take control. "You do it. Make yourself come."

Her hand snuck down between their bodies as she rubbed her clit with her finger until he felt her vibrate around his cock.

"Oh God."

He picked up the pace of his thrusts. She wanted rough, he'd give it to her rough. "Fuck yes. Perfect."

Seconds later, she squeezed his dick so hard he thought he'd lose it for sure. His balls drew up against his groin. Sweat popped out on his forehead. Surely his head would explode from the sheer force of his climax.

"Fuck!" Cum shot from the end of his cock into the latex condom. His whole body shook. He grasped her hips with his hands, knowing he'd leave bruises to mark her come morning, but he couldn't quite work up the ability to care beyond the satisfaction he'd marked her. *Mine.*

He shook his head as he slowly withdrew from her sweet warmth to dispose of the condom in the waste can next to the bed. *Where the hell did that thought come from? I sure in hell don't need a woman.*

Possessiveness whipped through him. She was his. At least until she left. He tapped her clit causing her to moan. "This is mine until you leave. Are we clear?"

"Yours?" The look of incredibleness flashing in her eyes made him feel even more possessive.

He wanted her, needed her with a fierceness he didn't know he possessed. "Yes, mine."

"Does that mean you're mine too, until I leave?" She stroked her hand down his chest. "It's only fair, yes?"

"All right. I'm yours until you leave, but don't think there will be anythin' beyond the time you're here. I don't want a woman in my life on any kind of permanent basis."

"I know, Jeff. You've made it abundantly clear." She scooted up to lean against the headboard on the bed. "Join me?"

"For a little bit. I can't stay. Mom is watching Ben and I told her I wouldn't be gone more than a couple of hours."

"Fuck and run, huh?"

"It's not like that, Terri. I don't want you to think I don't want to be here with you because I do, but my son comes before anyone."

"I know, Jeff. I appreciate the way you handle your son. It's endearing." She looked down at her body before she pulled the sheet up to cover herself. "I saw the blowup you had with your ex the other day. Kind of rough dealing with her, huh?"

"You have no idea." The bed dipped from his weight when he sat next to her. "I should have listened to my brothers when they tried to tell me she wasn't good for me."

"Hindsight is twenty-twenty."

"I know, but it doesn't make it any easier. Since we have Ben together, I have to deal with her for the rest of my life."

She stroked her hand down his arm. "I'm sorry."

"Somehow I get the feeling you wouldn't treat anyone badly. You seem like such a nice person."

Her nose wrinkled as she scrunched up her face. "I don't want to be nice. I want to be sexy, bold, and more woman than you can handle."

He laughed. The sound seemed raw and unused even to him. He didn't know how long it had been since he'd really laughed out loud. He always seemed to be in a bad mood except around Ben. Taking out his frustrations on his son wasn't an option so he kept his temper in check, but it took its toll. *Maybe I do need more adult company in my life other than my brothers and my parents.*

She sat forward, running her hand down his chest. "Stay a little while?"

"For another hour or so."

"I'm good with whatever time you can give me. Really."

He slipped beneath the sheet, curled his arm around her shoulder and tugged her in so her breasts pressed against his side. *Damn, she's got fabulous tits.*

Her arm snaked across his stomach to pull him closer to her side. "There. Better."

"Thanks for this, Terri."

"Thanks?"

"Yeah. I didn't realize how much I'd been missin' bein' with a woman until tonight. You've made me feel alive again, even if it's only for a little while."

"You need contact like this occasionally, Jeff." Her hand drifted down his abdomen. "You can't totally cut yourself off from being with a woman. It's a fundamental need for a man."

He kissed the top of her head. "Where'd you get so smart?"

"I'm a college graduate." A giggle escaped her lips as she brushed them across his chest. She tongued his right nipple, humming her appreciation when it hardened beneath her mouth. "I hope you brought more than one condom."

"I didn't want to be presumptuous."

"Presume all you want, cowboy. I need some lovin'."

With a quick flip, he had her on her back with her hands above her head. "Leave them there or I'll tie them."

Her eyes dilated. Her lips tilted up in a little smirk. "Yes, Sir."

"Good girl. I don't want to have to discipline you."

"But what if I want you to? I can be very bad."

Wow, he sure hadn't expected her to get into D/s play, but she jumped right into the role like she was made for it. "Spankin's can be arrange."

"Please."

"When I say so."

"Damn."

Her breasts tempted him to suck and nip. He wanted to drown in her smell, live in her eyes, and be a small part of her until their short time ended.

Chapter Six

The sun rose outside her cabin, pulling her from one of the best night's sleep she'd had in ages. She rolled over and propped herself up on her elbow to look at the sleeping man beside her. *So much for only a couple of hours.* The tattoo on his back left shoulder blade tempted her to touch while he lay sprawled on his stomach across her mattress. The dragon with the wide wingspan looked majestic and proud like the man it marked.

He wouldn't be happy about staying the entire night, but she didn't have the heart to wake him when he'd dozed off in the wee hours of the morning after they'd made love for the third time.

The warmth of the skin beneath the tattoo made her fingertips tingle and her pussy damp. How could she want him again? He must've turned her into some kind of slut or something if she wanted him again so soon.

"What?" Jeff shot up in the bed and looked around with a dazed expression. "What time is it?"

She glanced at the clock on the nightstand. "Six-thirty."

"Shit. I stayed all night? Why didn't you wake me?" He jumped out of the bed to grab his pants. "I need to get home. I need to get out of here before my brothers see me leavin' your place."

"Are you ashamed to have made love with me?" she asked, sitting up on the bed with the sheet clutched to her chest.

"No, darlin'. Not at all. I can't keep them from fuckin' around with the guests if I'm doin' it, now can I?"

"This isn't over is it?"

"Not by a long shot, but we need to keep it on the down-low. My mother will know since she stayed with Ben all night. I need to keep the others from findin' out."

"How do you plan to do that when I'm sure someone is probably up already?"

"I don't know." He raked his fingers through his hair. "Just pretend nothin' happened for now."

"I'm not going to hide the fact of our sleeping together, Jeff. There's nothing wrong with it."

"I didn't say there was."

She stood, bringing the sheet with her to hide her nakedness. "You're confusing me. You either don't care if your family knows or you do, which is it?"

"I don't want them to know because then all of my brothers will think it's open season on the single, beautiful women on the ranch."

"Then you don't want them to know. Fine. Don't let the door hit you on the ass on the way out."

"But Terri..."

"Don't but Terri me, mister. Get out!"

He threw his T-shirt over his head before he tugged on his boots.

Pain in the ass man!

When he pulled open the door, he glanced over his shoulder at her. "And don't bother comin' back, cowboy."

"You're mine."

"Bullshit, mister. You can't have it both ways. Either you want me or you don't. Either you do care if your family knows about us or you don't."

He returned to her side, wrapped his hand in her hair and slammed his mouth against hers. The kiss took her breath away, leaving her shaking and warm when he stepped back.

"This isn't over by a long shot, woman. I'll be back."

He shut the door quietly behind him, leaving her standing in the middle of the room with the sheet clutched to her chest and her head spinning from his kiss. She wiped at her mouth trying to erase the kiss, knowing full well she'd feel it for a long time to come.

"The gall of that man!"

Her cell phone rang on the nightstand bringing her out of her wandering thoughts of the disturbing cowboy who'd just left. "Hello?"

"Hi Terri. It's Bob Cole."

"Hi, Mr. Cole. How are you?"

"I'm fine. I'm just checking in with you to see how the information gathering is going."

"Great. I should have all the information you all need by the end of next week."

"Hmm. The end of next week?"

"Yes, sir."

"We need it sooner, Terri. We want to break ground on the new development by the beginning of next month. I need the information by the end of this week."

"But it's already Wednesday. I can't have it done before Friday."

"The contract depends on it being done before the end of this week."

She exhaled on a rush. "I'll do my best, sir, but I'm not promising everything by Friday."

"You'll have to or we'll have someone else finish the job. We like you, Terri, but we hired you to do a job and we expect it done satisfactorily on our time frame or no deal."

"But sir…"

"It's imperative we have the information. We hear some of the townspeople aren't happy about us coming in there so we need to get ground broke before they can organize a formal petition to stop us."

"I hadn't heard anything of the sort and I'm staying on one of the ranches out here to gather the details you need."

"Which ranch?"

"Thunder Ridge."

"Really. Interesting. One of their family members is rallying the townspeople to fight us on this. A," she heard paper shuffle before he came back, "Jeffery Young."

"Jeff?"

"You know him personally?"

Yeah, you could say a little personally. "Sort of. I've met him."

"What a great thing! Get close to him, Terri. We'll give you the extra time you need if you can find out a weakness with this guy. Something has to rub him the wrong way so we can stop his petition with the courts. The last thing we want is for him to manage to convince someone we are doing something wrong."

"You aren't, right? Everything is on the up and up?"

"Of course, it is Terri. We aren't doing anything illegal. Everything is above board."

She sighed. How in the hell would she be able to see Jeff and spy on him or give them something they could use against him? "Fine. I'll do what I can, but I can't promise anything."

"I'm sure you'll be able to find out something. He's got to have a weakness."

Yeah, his family.

"Remember, Terri. This could mean a lot of money for your business. The reputation of being involved in this project alone will help you become one of the big leaguers in Houston."

"I'll remember, Mr. Cole." The clock read seven. It would be breakfast soon. "I have to go. It's breakfast time."

"I'll call you again in a couple of days. You'll have the full two weeks you need so long as you help us with this little problem."

"I understand."

"Good. Talk to you soon."

"Bye." She flipped the phone shut with a decisive click. This wasn't going to be easy. Jeff already didn't trust a lot of people. If he found out she tricked him into divulging information to help his enemies, he would shut her out completely. "What to do. What to do." She tapped the phone against her lips. "Well, first I need a shower. I certainly can't go to breakfast looking like I just crawled out of bed." She glanced at her reflection in the mirror over the dresser. Well loved. Those were the words she'd use to describe her look. Her lips were slightly puffy from Jeff's passionate kiss before he left, her hair curled around her head in a wild disarray and her neck showed signs of whisker burn. She smiled. The look did wonders for her self-esteem. *A drop dead gorgeous cowboy fucked me five ways to Sunday. And I liked it!*

'Mine.' The growl of his words came back to make her blush. Did he really think of her as belonging to him? How should she feel about it? The thought brought goose bumps to her flesh. The sparkle in her eyes wasn't there before either. *Apparently, I really like the idea.*

With a smile on her lips, she grabbed clean clothes so she could take a nice shower before the breakfast bell clanged calling the guests to the main lodge. The non-descriptive bathroom in the guest cabins didn't have anything to write home about, but they were functional all the same. The white walls, white tile, white tub and white shower curtain left something to be desired. She leaned over the tub to turn on the water and let out a scream loud enough to wake the dead.

* * * *

Jeff had just returned from his cabin with Ben in tow as they were getting ready for the breakfast bell to be rung soon.

The blood curdling scream coming from Terri's cabin sent chills down his back. "Come on, Ben. Let's see what's up." The next scream brought him up on the porch at a dead run with Ben on his hip. "Terri?"

She screamed again.

"Terri, open the door."

"Jeff?"

"Open the door."

"It's open. Get in here!"

"What is it? What's wrong?"

"There's a big hairy bug in the tub."

"A what?"

"A big hairy bug. Get it out!"

He almost burst out laughing when he found her standing on the toilet lid with the sheet wrapped around her. "Ben. Stay out here by the bed. Okay, buddy?"

"Yes, Daddy."

"Where is it?"

"In the tub."

He held his chuckle in as he grabbed some toilet paper, pulled back the shower curtain and squashed the spider she called a big hairy bug. "There. It's gone."

"You're laughing at me."

"No, I'm not." He smiled. He couldn't help it. She looked so cute standing on the toilet shaking like a leaf in a wind storm. "It's all gone. You can take your shower now."

She slowly climbed down with the help from his hand. "Thank you. I hate bugs."

"You live in Texas and you hate bugs?"

A shiver rolled over her frame. "Yes."

She glanced through her lashes at him, making him want to kiss the daylights out of her. "We'll go now so you can shower."

He took Ben's hand before he headed for the door.

"Jeff?"

"Yeah?"

"Thank you."

"I'll slay your bugs any day, darlin'." He glanced over his shoulder, wishing he hadn't when his cock jumped to attention. Seeing her outlined by nothing but the sheet made him wish he hadn't left this morning. "See you at breakfast."

"She's purdy, Daddy."

"She sure is, buddy."

"Can she be my mama?"

"What makes you ask somethin' like that Ben? What about your real mama?"

"I don't think she loves me. I want a new mama."

Jeff squatted down in front of his son. "Buddy, you can't trade in your mama no matter how much you don't like what she does."

"But you don't like her anymore."

Jeff tipped his head back on his shoulders. How do you explain dealing with a bitter ex because you love your kid to a three-year-old? "Sometimes parents don't get along anymore and can't live together. It's not that I don't like her, we just can't be together anymore."

"I still like the purdy lady in the cabin."

"Me too, buddy. Me too." He stood and took Ben's hand again to head toward the main lodge. "Let's get some breakfast, huh? I think Grandma will be wondering where we are if we don't hurry up."

"The bell hasn't rung yet though."

"Well it will soon. We can get our juice earlier than everyone else."

"Yay!" Ben jumped as Jeff swung him up into his arms.

"Hey, bro!" Jackson came walking from the barn. "We missed you at the bonfire last night. Where did you run off to?"

"None of your business."

"Ah. A little more fun with Ms. Terri."

Jeff stopped at face his brother. "What I do on my private time is none of your damned business, Jackson. Back off."

"Easy, brother. I, for one, am thrilled you've found a nice lady. Terri seems to be a keeper."

"No one is a keeper for me. I'm done with women." Jeff glanced at Ben. "Buddy, go on into the house, okay?"

"All right, Daddy."

The minute Ben disappeared into the house, Jeff rounded on Jackson. "Back the fuck off."

"Sounded like you and Terri were havin' a good time by the pond. What happened?"

"One more word and I'll deck your ass."

Jackson put up his hands. "Whoa. I didn't mean nothin', Jeff. I hope you find a nice girl is all. The way Misha has run you through the ringer has us all worried about you. I think you'd do well to find a nice woman."

"I don't need a fuckin' woman. A quick lay is all I'm interested in. Gettin' tied up with a woman is the last thing I need. My son and my job are enough to satisfy me."

Jackson glanced over Jeff's shoulder as he tipped his hat. "Mornin', Ms. Terri."

"Morning, Jackson."

Terri walked around the two of them, but he grabbed her arm when she tried to scoot by. "Terri, wait."

"For what? You certainly don't give a shit about me or my feelings, Jeffery Young." She tried to yank her arm out of his grasp. "Let go."

"No." He dragged her around the corner of the building and pushed her against the wall of the house.

"You can't treat me like this."

"Listen to me."

"No. I'm done listening to your shit, Jeff. I get it. You don't want a woman in your life. You've told me enough damned times, I've memorized even the fluctuation of your words when you say it. A quick fuck. I got that part too." She pushed against his chest. "I don't need you either."

"It's not what it sounded like."

"The hell it wasn't!"

"Terri, please listen to me." He brushed his fingers against her cheek. "I didn't lie to you. My life hasn't been great and my ex is a bitch. I've been burned, darlin'. I don't have a heart left to give anyone even if I wanted to. All I have left, I give to my son. I live for him and only him."

"I know, Jeff." Tears streaked down her cheeks. "I never asked for your heart."

"I don't want you to be misled. I want us to be honest with each other from the start. What I told Jackson is the truth, but you knew everything from the beginning. Do I want you? Hell yes, baby. I want you more than my next breath, but I can't let another woman in only to be dragged through the mud again. I won't do it." He brushed his lips against her cheek, tasting her tears. "But if you want me to leave you alone, I will."

"No."

"No?" he asked, staring down into her beautiful green eyes as he cupped her face.

"I don't want you to leave me alone. I need you. God knows why I'm putting myself through this with you, but I want you too."

"Good." He stepped back after a quick peck on her lips. "I've decided I don't care whether anyone on the ranch knows we are together."

"You don't?"

"No. Hell, half of my brothers probably saw me leave this morning since most of the time they're up and in the barn by daybreak to get chores started." He wiped the remaining tears from her cheeks. "I won't put you in front of Ben though. I hope you understand."

"Of course, I do. He's your son."

"He's my life." He took her hand, threading his fingers with hers and headed for the door just as the breakfast bell clanged. "You can sit with the family today if you want or you can sit with your friends, but I want everyone to know about you. I don't want to sneak around anymore."

"You don't have to do that, Jeff. I know how much your privacy means to you."

"Yeah, but if you're with me, my brothers won't hit on you either."

She punched him in the arm. "Brat!"

He grabbed her and kissed her hard. "You'll pay for that later."

When they walked into the main lodge with the rest of the crowd of people, he waited for her to decide where she wanted to sit. He watched as she squared her shoulders and indicated with a tilt of her head she would sit with him at the family table. As they approached hand in hand, he garnered some weird looks from his family. "Everyone, this is Terri." He named off all of his siblings and his parents. "Joel and Mesa aren't here. They're still on their honeymoon until the end of the week."

"How fun."

"Welcome to the family table, Terri. You can sit next to Jeff and Ben at the end," Nina said with a twinkle in her eye.

"Thank you."

"Aren't you one of the guests?" Jacob asked, his eyes bloodshot from a probable hangover.

Jeff needed to talk to his brother to find out what the problem was now. It seemed Jacob was drinking more and more.

"Never mind, Jacob."

"But we ain't supposed to mess with the guests."

"Terri is here gathering information so she isn't really a guest," he answered his brother, hoping it would cut off the questions before Terri got uncomfortable or he had to tell the family her real purpose for being nearby.

"It doesn't matter. Welcome, Terri," Jeremiah said, taking her hand and kissing the back. "Let me know if you'd like to see more of the area while you're here. I'd be glad to take you around."

Jealousy reared its ugly head, making Jeff frown. He had no right to be jealous. "I've already taken her out, Jeremiah."

"Well, I'm sure there is *something* she hasn't seen."

"Back off," he growled, earning a huge grin from Jeremiah and the rest of his brothers too.

"Actually, can you show me the barn after breakfast?" she asked, looking between him and Jeremiah.

"What do you want to see the barn for?"

"I'd like to see the entire operation if I can."

His eyes narrowed on her. "I'm sure I can find something to interest you." *What the hell is she up to?*

"I'm sure you can." One eyebrow arched over her beautiful green eyes.

Did she have an ulterior motive for wanting to see the barn? Maybe she wants a roll in the hay. "All right."

"Great." She glanced down the table. "So who does what for the ranch?"

The table exploded into a beehive of conversation as everyone tried to talk at once. Terri laughed causing his balls to ache with want. He wanted nothing more than to take her back to her cabin and bounce the headboard against the wall some more.

They all managed to get their plates and sit back down before the talk started again. She got an earful of what everyone did on the ranch.

Jeff glanced at Jacob who seemed to be almost falling asleep in his breakfast. Had he been out all night drinking again? His brother seemed to have some issue. It was up to him as the eldest to find out what seemed to be the problem.

Jacob glanced up with a frown. "What?"

"You okay?"

"Yeah. Got in late."

"On a work day?"

"Back off, Jeff. I'm a big boy. I can handle a few late nights and some beers."

"I'm worried about you."

"I said back off!"

The entire group grew quiet.

"We can talk about this later."

"It's none of your damned business what I do on my off time. As long as I get the shit done around here, I can do whatever the hell I please." Jacob jammed his hat on his head and stomped out of the dining room.

"Well that went well," Nina said.

"Sorry, Ma. I'm worried about him." His gaze followed his brother's departure.

"We all are, Jeff, but bringing it up at the breakfast table wasn't a great idea."

"I didn't plan to. I just asked if he was okay. He exploded in the fiery temper he's known for." Jeff glanced at Terri concerned the ruckus might have given her the wrong idea of his family. She reached over to lay her hand on his thigh. A squeeze of reassurance let him know she didn't mind what happened. His heart flipped at the encouraging touch. No one had ever felt the need to do that kind of thing for him before. He held her hand in his for a brief moment before he released it to eat.

Breakfast ended without further incident, but he kept a leery eye on the female next to him.

"Finished?" she asked, getting to her feet.

"Yes."

"Let me grab the plates then. Did you want another cup of coffee before we head out?"

"Sure. Thank you." He glanced her way, determined to figure out this enigma of a woman who'd blown into his life like a tornado sure to destroy everything in her path.

"Black or cream and sugar?"

"Black is fine."

"Be right back," she said, her eyes twinkling with laughter. "Did you want more juice, Ben."

"Yes, ma'am."

"Please."

"Yes, ma'am, please," Ben repeated.

Terri smiled and bent to give him a hug before she picked up the plates. When she finished depositing the dishes into the dirty dish pan, she got him a cup of coffee and Ben more juice. "Here you go."

"You didn't want more?"

"I'm headed back to get me another cup right now."

Suspicion raced through his mind. Hadn't Misha started out sweet to everyone in her path too? He'd blown off her flirting with his brothers as her being nice rather than what it really was. She would have slept with any of them to become part of the family. She just happened to sucker him in with her dark hair and caramel eyes. Man, she'd done a number on him and still was if her threats yesterday meant anything. The bitch. If she tried to take Ben away, he'd kill her himself.

"What's got you looking so serious, cowboy?"

"Nothin'."

"Nothin', huh? It didn't look like nothin' to me. You looked ready to shoot someone."

"If I could, I would. My ex."

"Oh. Let's not talk about her, okay?"

"Good. I don't want to anyway."

The rest of the family had cleared out from the dining room, leaving the two of them and Ben finishing up.

"Can I go out and play, Daddy?"

"Wait until Grandma can go out with you. I have to get my chores done."

"Okay."

"I'll take him in a minute, Jeff. Let me finish up these bills first," his mother called from her office.

"Sure, Ma. We'll take him to the barn with us until you're ready." He finished his cup as Terri was finishing hers. "Ready?"

"Yes. I can't wait to see everything. I'm so excited!"

He laughed. Surely a bunch of cattle, hay, horses and animal droppings didn't seem so exciting, but then again, she lived in Houston where they had things like this, but you didn't see it much. "This stuff ain't that exciting."

"Sure it is, Jeff." She bounced on her toes like a little kid waiting for candy.

"All right. Off to the barn then." He helped Ben off the chair. "Come on, buddy."

"Can I hold your hand, Ms. Terri?"

"Oh, Ben. Of course you can, pumpkin."

Ben grinned from ear to ear as he took one adult hand in each of his. They headed out to the barn like a happy little family.

Oh fuck!

Chapter Seven

The barn smelled of hay, horse manure and leather. Smells she didn't like before, but she seemed to inhale them now with a new sense of worth or purpose, she wasn't sure which. Deceiving Jeff like this didn't sit well with her. Unfortunately, she had to with the hope things would work out for the best.

"What do you want to see?"

"Everything."

"Well, the horses are stabled here at night and in bad weather. Each has their own stall where we feed them and water them. We have a feed room and a tack room where we keep various things like grain or hay. The tack room is where we keep all the riding paraphernalia for the horses. You've already seen it."

"Yes. The lovely smell of leather."

"Daddy, can I show Ms. Terri my horse?"

"Sure, buddy."

Ben pulled her along to the small stall at the end. Inside, there was a beautiful palomino gelding. "Wow, he's gorgeous, Ben."

"I know. He's gold."

"What's his name?"

"Blackie."

She smiled when all she wanted to do was laugh. "Why did you call him Blackie when he's gold?"

"'Cause Daddy's horse is Blackie and I wanted to be like Daddy."

"Oh, I see."

"We call him Blackie and my horse Black Jack so we can tell them apart," Jeff said with a proud grin.

They two of them were so cute together, she couldn't help but smile.

"Will you be my new mama, Ms. Terri?"

"Ben, we already discussed this."

"I know, Daddy, but I thought I'd ask Ms. Terri for you."

"Sorry," he mouthed.

What do I say a three-year-old? "Honey, you have a mama already."

"I know, but I don't want her to be my mama anymore. I want you to be."

"Ben, listen. I can't be your mama. I don't live here with you and your new mama should live here so she can love you all the time."

"Okay."

The disappointment on the little boys face broke her heart.

"But we can be friends while I'm here."

"Yay!" Ben bounced in front of her on his little feet until she picked him up in her arms.

A quick kiss to her cheek almost made her cry. *What a great little boy.*

"Can we go for a ride, Daddy?"

"Not now, buddy. I have some work to get done. I need to organize the feed room." He glanced at Terri. "Would you mind keepin' an eye on him until my mom can take him back to the house?"

"Sure." She glanced at Ben. "How about we go dig in the dirt for a while?"

"Can I get my trucks, Daddy?"

"Of course you can, Ben."

"You have dump trucks?"

Ben nodded quickly.

"Awesome. I love playing with dump trucks."

"I have lots of different ones too." He squirmed to get down.

"He keeps them in the feed room," Jeff said, following the running little boy down the dirt aisle of the barn.

Two cowboys in their finery. Ben had his little hat, tiny jeans and miniature cowboy boots where Jeff had the mighty fine grownup version. The man looked delicious. His ass looked tight in the Wranglers. *Damn.*

"You comin'?"

"I wish," she mumbled, following the man as she admired his backside.

Ben grabbed the box with his trucks in it, struggling to hold all of them. "Let me help."

"Okay."

She took the box out of his arms. "Will you hold my hand and show me where you play?"

"Yes, ma'am."

With a quick glance at his beaming father, she winked and said, "After you, sir."

Ben led her back down the aisle of the barn, around the outside and to a small dirt mound next to the wall. Shaded by a large tree she wasn't familiar with, she made a mental note to include it in her findings for the development company although she wasn't sure she'd get a lot accomplished on her mission by playing trucks with a three-year-old. Today, she didn't care. Today was about playing and having fun. Later, she'd worry about details like how much feed they went through, where they bought their stock and how many guests they had in a month. She didn't know how that would help the land developers, but she figured the more information she had on Thunder Ridge Guest Ranch, the better.

For the next hour, she played alongside the little boy in the dirt pile, until his grandmother came outside.

"What are you two doin' over there?" Nina asked, coming to a stop next to them.

"We are building houses, Gram."

"Are you now? Is Ms. Terri helping you build those houses?"

"Yes, ma'am. She draws them on paper and then the constuction man put them together."

"Oh?"

Shit. "I'm an architect by trade."

"Really? We've thought about adding on to the main lodge at times, maybe you can talk to me about square footage, building plans and permits one of these days before you leave."

"I would love to."

"Pick up your trucks, Ben. It's time to wash up."

"Aw, Gram."

"Come on, little man. You need to come inside so Ms. Terri can talk to your daddy. I believe she has some questions for him."

The twinkle in Nina's eye didn't go unnoticed. What was the woman up to? Playing matchmaker? Surely, she didn't think anything could come of her short stay here at the ranch? "Thanks, Nina. I do need to talk to him about some things."

Nina patted her on the hand. "There ya go. I knew you two needed some alone time."

Terri shook her head in denial. "It's not like that. I need to make some notes on a project I'm working on."

"Of course you do, honey."

Terri rolled her eyes. Apparently, Nina wanted her son hooked up with someone hopefully better than his ex. *You're spying on him. Does that make you better?* She bit her lip to keep from blurting out her purpose. She didn't like lying to these people.

"Come on, Ben. Let's go inside."

Nina walked away with Ben in tow, leaving Terri with the box of trucks at her feet. She grabbed it in her arms and headed back inside the barn to find Jeff. He stood inside the feed room with a clipboard in his hands as he scratched his head in apparent frustration.

"What's wrong?"

"Huh? Oh, hi." He pushed his hat back down on his forehead, and then jotted down some numbers. "I can't figure out where all the feed is going. We seem to be going through a lot more than normal this month."

"I wonder why."

"Well it could be because it's been rather dry so far. I'll have to ask Joey if he's been doubling up on feed or something for some reason."

"How much do you go through a month normally?"

He narrowed his eyes as he looked at her for a moment. It took him a second to answer and she hoped he wouldn't get suspicious about her questions. "Several tons of both hay and grain."

"How many animals do you have?"

"We have fifty horses and thousands of head of cattle. We don't feed the cattle much out of the stores unless the grazing is bad. They have round bales of hay we feed them to supplement their grazing."

"Sounds like a huge operation."

"It is. With the guests and running the cattle operation, it's a big job."

"I can't imagine."

"What are you getting at, Terri."

"Me? Nothing, why?"

"Why all the questions? I thought you had everything you needed when I took you out to the property lines."

"I did. I mean, I do. I want to spend some time myself learning about the operation though for my own information. It has nothing to do with the developers, Jeff." She cringed. Lying to him put a bad taste in her mouth.

"Why don't I necessarily believe you?"

"I don't know. I haven't given you a reason to distrust me."

"I distrust all women so it's not just you."

"I wish you didn't have such a terrible view of women. You've been hurt. I get it, but you know not all women are like your ex. You should think hard on that before you mistrust everyone."

He put the clipboard down on the bale of hay and pulled her close. "True." He brushed her lips with his. "I want you. Right now."

"Now?"

"Yeah. We can lock the door. Ever fucked in a tack room on a bale of hay?"

"Can't say that I have."

"This can be your first," he said, trailing his lips down her neck.

"You're very persuasive, you know." Shivers raced down her arms as she grabbed a fistful of his shirt. The snaps gave way with a forceful tug of her hands. "I love your chest."

He lifted her shirt over her head before he unsnapped her bra and drew it down her arms. "I love your tits."

She rolled her eyes.

"What?"

"Women don't like the word tits. It's vulgar."

"What do you call them?"

"Breasts or boobs."

He cupped her bare breasts in his palms, thumbing her nipples to hard little points. "I like your boobs, then."

"Men."

"They fit perfectly in my palms."

"They're too small."

"No they aren't. They're perfect."

He ran his tongue over one nipple, pulling a gasp from her lips. She hadn't realized her nipples were so sensitive to his touch. "Mmm."

"Like that?"

"Oh, hell yeah."

He worked the button at her waist loose while he continued to bite at her nipple. Her jeans fell to a puddle at her feet.

"My shoes."

"Up on the bale and I'll pull them off. I want to eat you anyway."

Her pussy clenched as desire raced through her.

"Let me grab a blanket. It might be a bit itchy." An older horse blanket lay in the corner. He grabbed it and spread it on the hay bale. "This would be better in your bed or mine, but I'm so damned hard for you, I can't wait."

"Just fuck me, Jeff. No prelims, just raw sex."

He grabbed a condom from his wallet, unbuckled his pants, shoving them to the floor in his haste and then rolled the condom down his impressive cock. "Are you wet?"

"Damn right, I'm wet. I've been dripping since you walked down the aisle after Ben with your tight ass in those jeans. You are one impressive cowboy, cowboy."

The head of his cock bumped at her opening.

"Sweet Baby Jesus." He slowly pushed his cock inside her pussy, dragging out every inch in sweet agony. His thumb found her clit, pulling a moan from between her lips. It felt wonderful, magnificent. She lost the ability to think as he moved in and out of her pussy.

"God, you feel like heaven."

"Harder, Jeff."

His pace increased. Heat crawled up from her toes. She was going come and come hard. "Kiss me."

He pulled her in for the most devastating kiss she'd ever had in her life, just in time for her body to explode in a climax big enough to curl her toes where they rested around his hips.

The kiss broke as he panted her name over and over until he climaxed in a rush.

"Jeff?"

"Shit!"

"Seriously? Who the hell is calling you now?"

"Jonathan."

"Fuck." Jeff scrambled to ditch the condom and right his jeans so he could answer his brother while she quickly grabbed hers from the pile to slip on. They were going to be caught red-handed fucking in the stock room.

"Hang on, Jonathan. I'll be right out."

"Are you in the tack room?"

"Stay where you are," Jeff growled as he tucked his shirt into his pants. "You dressed?" he whispered glancing her way while she struggled to get her bra back on.

"Does it fucking look like it?"

"I'll meet him out there so you have time to finish."

"Thanks." Hell, she still needed to get her pants back up. Guys had it so much easier. Whip it out, fuck like bunnies and stuff it back in.

Jeff closed the door behind him, but she could still hear the voices.

"What's up?"

"I needed to ask you something about the program to keep track of the feed so you aren't doing it all by paper anymore."

"Okay, what?"

"Can we go into the tack room? I need to see how big the sacks of grain are so I can—"

"No."

"Why the hell not?"

"It's a mess."

"What? Seriously? Who the fuck cares if it's a mess?"

"I do. I've got shit all over in there. I don't want you messing with my system."

"System? You don't have a damned system, Jeff. I need to see the sacks."

The next thing she knew, the door flew open and she came face to face with Jonathan.

"Oh."

"Hi."

"Hello." His face turned bright red as he dropped his gaze to the hay covered floor. "Sorry. I didn't mean to interrupt."

"You didn't," she said, holding back laughter as she put her shoes back on her feet.

"I'll uh…get those later, Jeff."

"You do that, Jonathan."

Jonathan took off at a dead run out of the barn, his face still bright red even from where she sat on the hay bale.

"Sorry. I guess I should have hid or something."

"No, it's fine. It's not like he's a virgin or somethin'. He's kind of shy, is all. He takes care of our website and computer stuff around here. He's building me a program to keep track of all of this without having to do it on paper."

"Sounds interesting." She stood in front of him now, wishing they'd had more time. It had been so great having him sleep beside her all night, but she knew it wouldn't happen again anytime soon. Ben took priority over everything he did, as it should be for a father. It just made her realize with kids, personal time took a backseat to the needs of the child. "What else can you tell me about the operation?"

"We have six guest rooms outside of the man lodge house. Ten more rooms upstairs from the family quarters where my parents sleep."

"Sounds like you can take a lot of guests."

"Yeah. We have a few double rooms upstairs where families can have two rooms or two of the cabins have connecting doors for families too."

"Have you ever been in a lawsuit for an accident on the ranch?"

He frowned. "What kind of question is that?"

"Just curious is all."

"Well, not that it's any of your business, but no, we haven't. Keeping our guests safe is a huge priority for us. We make sure everyone who rides is given instructions beforehand. They are screened to make sure their riding ability is good before they ever get on a horse. If they've never been on one before, they are given their own riding lessons."

"I didn't mean anything by it, Jeff. I would think this would be a high risk operation for liability purposes is all. I'm thinking of you."

"An accident could shut us down."

"I'm sure."

Her cell phone jingled in her pocket, but she planned to ignore it. She knew who it was without looking since she'd assigned a specific ringtone to the developers. The last thing she needed to do was answer it in front of Jeff.

"Aren't you gonna get that?" he asked, propping himself up against the doorframe with his arms over his chest, looking all the more enticing with his clothes back in place.

"I know who it is. It's my mother. I'll call her back in a bit." She stepped forward and ran a fingernail down his chest. "Is there another time we can get together, maybe?"

"I don't know."

"What about at your place?"

"I have Ben."

She fiddled with the buttons on his shirt as she glanced up through her lashes. "I know, Jeff. I wouldn't ask you to put anyone in front of his needs. He's your son."

Her cell phone jingled again.

"Sounds important. Maybe you should answer it."

"I guess so." She glanced at the screen. Yep, the developers. "It's almost lunch time anyway so I'm going to head back to my room to freshen up. I'll see you in the main lodge."

"Okay." He kissed her quickly on the lips.

A simple brush of his mouth against hers, but her panties felt drenched from the small touch.

The smile she gave him was genuine. She really liked him. Probably a little too much.

Chapter Eight

Terri took the phone from her pocket as she opened the door to her cabin, to call the developers back. Annoyance rushed through her. She had a job to do, but they certainly didn't seem to want to let her do it.

The phone redialed with a push of her finger.

After the receptionist rattled off her greeting, Terri asked to speak to one of the partners. Mr. Cole picked up the line. "Terri, we need an update."

"I don't have an update for you. I haven't learned anything really. It hasn't even been half a day."

"My source on the counsel has informed me the committee has all but agreed with the idiots at Thunder Ridge to postpone the land development until they can do more research on land impact. I need something right now. What about the operation itself? Surely you've been able to find out some information on their financial situation?"

"I know they haven't had any lawsuits." She frowned. What did all of this have to do with the development and building houses on their property? It almost sounded like they wanted to put Thunder Ridge out of business if they could.

"Well maybe we'll need to work on that then."

"What do you mean? These are nice people."

"Don't get attached, Terri. We're in business to make money. We need more property to make more money. It's as simple as that."

"It's just a family run guest ranch with some cattle on it. They are no threat to you."

"Everyone in the area is a threat to us."

"Why?"

"We need more land. We don't care how we get it."

"I don't understand?"

"Just get the information we need or you won't have a job when this is through. Maybe not even a company to go back to." *Click.*

What the fuck?

"He didn't seriously just threaten me, did he?"

"My guess is, yes, he did."

She spun around to find Jeff at her open door.

"You left your underwear in the feed room. I thought I'd bring them back before someone else found them."

The concern in his eyes had feelings blooming that shouldn't be there. Feelings for him would complicate things. "It's not what it sounds like."

He moved inside the room and shut the door. "Explain it to me then. Is someone threatening you?"

"I…"

"If there is something I can do, tell me. I don't like the thought of someone hurting you for any reason."

"Why?"

"I've grown kind of attached to you while you've been here. If someone is hurting you and I can help, then let me."

"It's nothing, Jeff. Really. I can handle it."

"Are you sure?"

"Yeah." She took the underwear from his hand. "Thanks for bringing these back." She tossed them on the bed. "Going commando isn't what it's cracked up to be."

"No, it's not. I've done it a time or two myself."

"Have you now."

"Yep."

She glanced down at the straining material of his jeans. "Like now?"

"No, but somethin' is wantin' to come out and play." He glanced at his watch. "We have about fifteen minutes."

"I think we should wait."

"Why?" he asked, his eyes wide with confusion.

"You might be able to get off in fifteen minutes, but we women like to take it a little slower sometimes. The quick fuck in the feed room should have satisfied you for a little bit, cowboy."

"All right."

The little pout on his mouth made her smile. A quick nibble on his lips brought the reaction she wanted as he moaned softly and took the kiss to explosive in record time. When they finally came up for air, he groaned as he pressed his forehead against hers.

"Tonight. My place."

"I thought you didn't want to do anything with Ben there?"

"He'll be asleep by seven. We can have the whole night. Bring your car so you can leave whenever you want. You can follow me home after supper tonight." He grasped her butt to pull her closer. "Ever had a man in your ass, honey?"

"Nope."

"Want to?"

Her butt cheeks clenched at the thought. She'd always wanted to try, but she hadn't had the nerve or the trust in someone to allow them to go that far. "Maybe."

"Don't worry. You'll love it and if you don't we don't have to pursue it any further."

The rock hard chest beneath her breasts made her nipples ache for friction. She wanted to run them all over the front of his shirt.

"Quit lookin' at me like that."

"Like what?"

"Like you'd strip me to bare skin and ride my hips into tomorrow if we had time."

"I do?"

"Yep."

"Sounds good to me." The lunch bell clanged. "Well damn." He laughed, rich and deep. *Damn, I like his laugh.* "You should laugh more often."

"You know, darlin', I've laughed and smiled more since I met you than I have in several years."

"I'm glad I could help."

"You've done wonders for me." He hugged her, and then opened the door. "I love you."

What the hell? She stumbled over her feet before she glanced up into his eyes.

"I didn't mean that how it sounded. "I meant I love bein' around you. You've brought a lot of joy into my life I haven't had for a long time."

He took her hand as he shut the door behind them.

"Good. You had me scared there for a minute."

"I'm glad I let you in, Terri. I'll just be sorry when it has to end."

"Yeah, me too, Jeff. Me too.

* * * *

He mentally kicked himself in the ass as they walked to the main lodge for lunch. *What the fuck was I thinking? That had to be the stupidest thing I've ever said in my life, well maybe except for when I talk to Misha.*

Luckily, Terri seemed to go with his explanation because he sure as hell didn't have anything else to say. *I love you. Stupid, man. Really stupid.*

They walked through the doors into the chaos of the noonday meal. Several new guests had come in during the morning hours it appeared. "Do you want to eat with us at the family table again?"

"Of course," she gushed and he frowned.

God, I hope she isn't taking this too seriously. Maybe they needed to slow this shit down. Hell, he wasn't sure anymore himself. He seemed to by flying by the seat of his pants and the fuckers were on fire for this woman.

They greeted everyone at the table with hello. His brothers seemed to be keeping a secret with all the smiles and looks their way. Hopefully, they didn't think there was something else going on between him and Terri. He'd have to straighten them out before too long. His mother played matchmaker all the damned time with her sons, but he wasn't gonna to fall for the whole lot of them trying to hook him up. He didn't need their help. He was gettin' laid on a semi-regular basis while Terri hung around and that suited him just fine, thank you very much.

"Why is everyone grinnin'?" she asked quietly.

"This is the second meal you've shared at the family table. They're probably gonna be askin' about church bells soon."

"Hell no," she hissed.

"My thoughts exactly."

"Should I tell them?"

"No, let them wonder. It's a game. Think of it that way."

Her green eyes twinkled with mirth. "Oh, I like pulling the wool over their eyes. I think it'll be fun."

"Yep."

The guests were served so everyone at the family table got up to get their food. "Can I get you some coffee or lemonade?" he asked.

"Sure. Lemonade sounds great."

When they returned to the table and sat down to eat, conversation sped around the table in varying degrees, everything from problems on the ranch to issues with the cattle from the morning rounds.

"Jeff, I found a couple of cattle down in the south pasture. The water trough was empty again."

"What? I fixed it two days ago."

"There's a big hole. Looks like a bullet hole to me."

"Do we have to start patrolling the fence line again? Jesus."

"Jeffery."

"Sorry, Ma, but this is nuts. You'd think we were livin' in the frickin' eighteen hundreds. Worryin' about cattle rustlers is crazy."

"We'll deal with it, son," James added before he took a bite of his food.

"We don't have the man power to have to patrol the fence twenty-four/seven, Dad."

"I know we don't, but we'll figure somethin' out. First thing, move the water trough to behind a rock so it's not visible from the fence line. At least it will make it more difficult for someone to take potshots at it."

"I'll take care of it, Dad," Joshua said.

"Thanks, Josh. I've got some things to work on in the barn this afternoon," Jeff answered.

"Yeah, we know," Jonathan added with a smirk and a look at Terri.

Great. I hope the whole damned bunch doesn't know about our tryst. "Jonathan," he growled, hoping his brother would take the hint.

"There must have been possum in the feed room earlier. Did ya get it?"

Jeff wanted to punch his brother. "Yeah, I got it."

The whole table erupted in laughter.

"What did I miss?" Terri asked, apparently not getting the joke.

"Never mind, darlin'. I'll explain later. Just ignore shithead over there."

"It's kind of hard to ignore being the butt of a joke, Jeff."

He leaned over and whispered, "Apparently, Jonathan has informed the whole family of what happened in the barn between us earlier."

She bit her lips as her eyes closed. Red swept up her neck, splashing across her face in a bright hue as everyone laughed.

"Enough!" James shouted. "You boys should be ashamed to treat a guest this way."

"Sorry, Terri. I didn't mean to embarrass you." Jonathan sounded trite, but Jeff wasn't sure it was genuine. Either way, he planned to kick his brother's ass for him after lunch.

She opened her eyes and smiled. "It's fine."

Wow. She's a better person than I am.

They finished the rest of the meal without any more hassles from his family. Jeff picked up their plates when they finished, taking them to the dirty dish pan. He grabbed three desserts on his way to returning to the table. The rest of the family cleared out leaving him alone with Terri and Ben. They seemed to be doing that a lot since she'd arrived.

"Do you have somethin' you can do this afternoon? I've got work to get done." The spoon disappeared between her tempting lips, making him want to stick something else between those plump lips. Maybe tonight he could get her to suck him. Just for a minute. He'd probably explode the minute she took him in her mouth. He shook his head to clear the erotic thoughts. The last thing he needed was a raging hard-on to work with this afternoon. Of course, throwing some hay bales would quickly deflate it.

"Sure. If you don't mind, I'd like to talk to some of your brothers about some of the other stuff they do around the ranch."

"Why's that?" he asked, suspicion crowding his thoughts. She did work for the developers trying to take over everything around Bandera.

She shrugged as she took another bite. "I'm curious. I've never been on a working cattle ranch. I'd like to know more about each man's job on the ranch."

Her thigh plastered against his waylaid his thoughts again. *Damn.* He needed to get his mind out of bed with Terri and back on work. "There is a hay ride this evening if you'd like to go. Dad does a great informational thing on the longhorn cattle we have."

"Great! I'd love it. He seems like an interesting person."

"He's been doin' this a long time."

After she finished her dessert, she pushed the small cup away as she licked her lips. He so wanted to taste the chocolate confection on her mouth. He leaned in ready to do exactly what he thought until Ben squeezed between them. "Hey, buddy."

"Can Ms. Terri come over our house tonight?"

"What for?"

"I wanna show her my room."

Jeff raised an eyebrow in a questioning look trying to convey to her this would give them a perfect opportunity for a night of lovemaking at his place.

"Sure, Ben," she answered. "I'd love to see your room."

"Okay. Off with Gram, Ben. I've got work to do and so does Ms. Terri." He stood and helped Terri to her feet. "I'll walk you back to your cabin."

"You don't have to do that. How about if I get with Jonathan and Jeremiah so I can get the business side of things?"

"There's an office by the check-in office where Jeremiah works on the books. I'll take you there before I head to the barn."

"Thanks."

They rounded the corner of the main lodge just in time for the front door to open and close by itself. He rolled his eyes. He hoped she didn't have a problem with ghosts since they had a few of them running around the ranch, especially in the main lodge since it used to be a brothel. They didn't have a lot of problems in the cabins, but the main house had its share. The local cowboy who haunted the place kept things lively, but the real draw for a lot of folks was the noisy couple upstairs. Even Mesa had a run in with them when she stayed there.

"Did that door just open and close by itself?"

"It's ghost," Ben whispered in a loud voice.

"Ghost?" she asked, her eyes wide with wonder.

"It's nothin'. Probably the wind," Jeff answered before Ben could go further. "Off to see Gram, Ben."

"Okay, Daddy." Ben scrambled into Nina's office as he rounded the corner to show Terri where Jeremiah's office was.

"Here you go." He knocked on the door and heard a muffled greeting. He opened it to find Jeremiah bent over his desk with papers scattered everywhere. The office looked like a bomb had gone off in there. "Damn, Jeremiah. I don't see how you can get anythin' done with this mess."

"I know exactly where everything is so just back off."

He held up his hands. "I brought Terri in to talk to you. She has some questions."

"Sure. Come on in, Terri. There's a chair there in the corner if you'd like to sit."

"Thank you," Terri answered, grabbing the wooden chair from its spot to drag it closer to the desk.

"I'll leave you two alone then. I'll see you at supper, Terri."

"Of course."

"Have fun and behave yourself, Jeremiah."

"Always, brother."

He closed the door, but stopped with his hand on the doorknob. *Why was she so interested in the financial aspect of the ranch? Things weren't quite addin' up with Terri Kennedy. Maybe if I get to know her better, she'll tell me what she's up to.*

Jeff shook his head as he walked out the doors headed for the barn. What to do with her, he wasn't sure, but keeping an eye on her seemed to be a priority now. Her inquiries into things going on at the ranch worried him. A talk between him and Jeremiah would be in order after work had been completed for the day. He hoped she wasn't up to no good. Trust came hard for him and he'd begun to trust her. He just hoped it wasn't misplaced.

Jacob came out of the tack room, stumbling slightly.

"Are you okay?"

"I'm fine."

The smell of alcohol coming from his brother's breath almost knocked Jeff down.

"Jacob, are you drunk?"

"No. I wish to hell I was."

Jeff grabbed his brother's arm and hauled him into the tack room. "What the fuck is goin' on with you? You've been drinking in here?"

"Fine. Yeah, I've been drinkin'. It's none of your fuckin' business what I do." Jacob shoved Jeff back, yanking his arm out of his brother's grasp. Without the added support, he stumbled again.

"We're here for you, Jacob. But, listen, man. This has to stop."

"Just leave me the fuck alone." Jacob tumbled backward into a chair sitting near the desk they used to do some of the tack repairs on.

"Tell me."

"You don't fuckin' care about any of us! Why the hell should I tell you anything."

"Because you're drinkin' way too much. Here it is the middle of the damned day on a weekday and you're drunk off your ass. Were you drunk at breakfast too?"

"Yeah, I was!" Jacob straightened himself in the chair and he tried to rise. Jeff slammed him back down with a hand on his shoulder.

"Jacob, what's gotten into you? You didn't used to drink like this."

"It doesn't matter. I ain't tellin' you anything so back the fuck off, Jeff. What I do isn't your business."

"Everythin' at this ranch is my business. Get it through your head brother and we'll be fine. The drinkin' has to stop. I mean now, Jacob."

"Fuck you." Jacob stumbled to his feet as he pushed his way past Jeff.

Jeff grabbed his arm, but Jacob yanked it back. "Come on, Jacob. Talk to me."

"Leave me alone, Jeff. The problems I have are none of your business."

"I want to help you."

"You're too wrapped up in your latest woman to care about me or anyone else on this ranch."

"Don't bring Terri into this. She ain't got nothin' to do with you or me."

"Why the hell not? She's another slut…"

Jeff pulled back his fist and hit Jacob on the chin, laying him flat out on the floor of the tack room. "Terri is a good woman. She's not a money-hungry female after this ranch or what money she can get from me. She has her own business and is working an important job. Keep your filthy opinions to yourself."

"What's goin' on here," their father said, stopping in the doorway.

"Jacob is drunk again. He's been drinkin' on the job. He's probably got some booze hidden in here somewhere so he can sneak a drink whenever he comes in."

"Is this true, Jacob?"

Jacob tried to sit up. "I was drunk last night. Today, I'm hung over. That's all, Dad."

"You can smell the alcohol on his breath."

Their father held out his hand to help Jacob to his feet. Jeff wasn't fooled. He knew his father planned to smell Jacob's breath for himself.

"Jacob, go to your place. You need to sleep off whatever you've been drinking."

"But, Dad?"

"But nothin'. I don't want to hear another word from you."

"I'm thirty years old. If I want to get plastered, I can."

"Not while you're workin' this ranch, son." Their father turned him toward the door. "Go on. We'll talk later about this."

Jacob stumbled out the door, almost falling on his face as Jeff and their father stood by to watch.

"What are we gonna do with him, Dad?"

"I'm not sure, Jeff. I wish I knew what caused him to start drinkin'."

"I don't know either."

"Have you heard of woman problems or anythin' with him?"

"No. I know he had a girlfriend not too long ago, but I thought their split was a mutual thing." Jeff shook his head. "Maybe he took it harder than I thought."

"Maybe, but I don't think Jacob was in love with her. Do you?"

"He might have been, Dad. I know he never brought her around here. I saw her with him a couple of times at the bar. They seemed chummy, but he sure didn't act like he was in love." He stepped back inside the tack room when Jacob went inside his trailer. His wasn't far from the house to the back of the garden area. "I sure ain't an expert on the subject though."

James laughed, and then sobered. "Sorry, son. I didn't mean to make fun of you, but you sure aren't an expert with your track record."

"Misha was a huge mistake even though she gave me Ben."

"He's the light of our lives, Jeff. You know that, right?"

"Yeah, Dad, I do. He's my pride and joy. I love him with all my heart."

James took a seat on the edge of the desk. "What's going on between you and Terri Kennedy?"

"Nothin', why?"

"You seem pretty familiar with each other for nothin' goin' on," his father said, folding his arms over his chest.

"She's a great gal. We're havin' a little fun together until she leaves."

"Yeah, Joel said the same thing until Mesa left to go back to Los Angeles."

"Joel fell in love with her in like a week, Dad. That's not normal."

"When love finds you, son, you don't have a choice in the matter. Not if it's real love."

"Well, I don't plan to fall in love with anyone. Women are more of a pain in the ass than their worth."

One eyebrow rose over James' left eye. "True, but the love you get in return more than makes up for the hassle you go through."

"I don't think so."

"With the right woman, it is."

"Hmm." Jeff took a bridle down from the wall and fiddled with the bit. "Did I tell you I had to save Terri from a bug in her tub this mornin'?"

"No." James laughed. "I thought she was from Houston. Surely she knows about the bugs in Texas."

"I woulda thought so but she apparently doesn't do bugs." Jeff laughed too. It had been rather funny to see her standing on the toilet wrapped in a sheet.

"I haven't seen you laugh in a long time, son. I think she's good for you."

"Don't get your hopes up. It's nothin' permanent."

"What's she doin' here anyway? I think there is more to her visit than meets the eye. She's interested in things most normal guests aren't."

"I'm keepin' an eye on her."

"Why?"

"Don't judge her, okay? I don't think she means harm, but I can't be sure." Jeff laid the bridle on the desk. "She's an architect for the development firm who bought the land next to ours. They plan on putting a housing project in there. She's doing some research on the area to get an idea of what types of houses she'll be designing for them to build."

"That's serious stuff."

"I know."

"She's in talkin' to Jeremiah." James rapped his knuckles on the desktop. "I don't like her knowing our financial situation, Jeff."

"I don't think Jeremiah is stupid enough to tell her anything pertinent. I hope she's gettin' general information is all."

"I'll talk to Jeremiah after she leaves to find out what exactly he told her," his father said.

"Those money-hungry land barons could be trying to put us out of business."

"Yeah, and she'd be helping them."

"I don't see how gathering information to figure out what kind of houses to design would be helping to put us out of business."

"Why else would she need financial information or anything along those lines?"

"I don't know."

"Why don't you ask her?"

"How the hell do I do that, Dad? In between orgasms I say, *tell me what you're up to, Terri. I need to know if you're trying to ruin my family.* Somehow it doesn't come across to me as pillow talk."

"You'll know what to do, son. You always do."

Chapter Nine

Terri watched Jeff eat each morsel with finesse. She wasn't sure how he made eating look sexy, but he sure did. The tines of the fork slipped between his full lips, tempting her to want to taste him or have him taste her. He'd been quiet since they'd met up for dinner. Conversation flowed around them from all of his brothers, but he didn't seem interested in talk this evening. Ben kept up a lively conversation with his grandmother about their activities for the day. Terri smiled while she listened to him.

Jeff finally broke the silence between them as he leaned over and whispered, "Are we still going to meet later?"

"I hope so."

"Do you want to?"

"Yes."

When she glanced up, she met the narrowed gaze of James. Why she earned the distrust of the monarch of the family, she wasn't sure. She didn't like it though. She hated having anyone mistrust her or question her motives. *Why shouldn't they? I've been mysterious the whole time I've been here, gathering information on them that really isn't any of my business. By passing this along, will it hurt this family in the long run? I don't know.*

"You okay?" Jeff asked.

"Yes, why?"

"You looked concerned."

"Your father seems to dislike me for some reason."

"He doesn't dislike you. He doesn't know you, how could he dislike you?"

"I don't know." She glanced at Jeff. "Did you tell him why I'm here?"

Jeff blushed and dropped his gaze to his plate.

"You did. No wonder he doesn't trust me," she whispered out the side of her mouth. "What did you tell him?"

"Your reason for being here was to collect data for the developers."

"True. What else?"

"Nothin'." He finished his plate and pushed it away. "We'll talk more about this later."

"Fine."

"Ben, are you done, buddy?"

"Yes, Daddy."

"I'll get your dessert."

She looked up to see him staring at her.

"Would you like something?"

"The apple crisp looks good."

"I'll grab one for you while I'm up."

"Thanks." When she glanced across the table to Jeff's dad, the older man smiled. She hoped that meant he'd give her a chance to explain. Of course, explaining might mean telling him what she really had up her sleeve.

"Here you go," Jeff said, sitting the small cup down in front of her.

The apples, cinnamon and crispy granola melted on her tongue with each bite she took. They had the best desserts at this ranch. If she lived here all the time, she'd weight a lot more than she did now. Not that she was a skinny person by any means. Her hips were too big, she had a bit of a stomach roll and her boobs were too small for her. Jeff didn't seem to mind though, which was a good thing.

"We can watch a movie with Ben until he falls asleep which is usually within the first hour or so."

"Sounds good."

Terri glanced around the table, meeting several of his brother's gazes. She didn't like the looks they were giving her. *Had they somehow heard about her real job?*

"You didn't tell your brothers, right?"

"No, just my father, but you have to admit your behavior has been rather suspicious."

"Suspicious how?"

"Most guests don't want to talk to the financial planner of our group. I don't know if Jeremiah might have told them what things you were asking him. What did you ask, by the way?"

"Nothing much."

"I don't want to discuss this in front of the family."

Her dessert was already gone.

"Shall we go?"

"Uh, sure." *Does Jeff suspect something? I don't like the way he seems to hint at a conversation concerning my information gathering and then goes off on another topic. Should I tell him what I'm doing? Think Terri, think.* "Is everything okay, Jeff?"

"We'll discuss it at my place."

Oh, I hate when people do that! It drove her nuts to be put off. "Are you sure you don't want to discuss it now?"

"Not in front of my family."

"Oh."

They put their dishes in the dirty dish pan, took Ben's hands and walked out of the door toward his truck. "Let me grab my keys and purse from my cabin."

"Good idea."

She turned left to take the path to her door, unlocked the cabin and walked inside. She debated on whether to change into something sexy. At least sexy underwear? No, she really didn't have time. He wouldn't wait forever and she already planned on having sex with him tonight. Before or after their talk, she wasn't sure. *Maybe before. If he gets wind of what I'm really up to, there may not be any sex.*

Putting off their *talk* sounded like a good idea.

With her purse and keys in hand, she shut the door to her cabin before she checked the lock to make sure it was secure. Jeff stood by his truck's passenger door buckling Ben into his car seat. The way Jeff treated Ben said a lot about the man. He cared. He might not care for her, at least not in any meaningful way, but in his own way, he cared. She'd seen it when he asked about her phone call and someone threatening her.

"Ready?" he called as she approached her car.

"Yeah."

"Good. Follow me. I'll be slow so I don't lose you."

"Is it far?"

"Nope. Just over the ridge on the other side of the main road."

"Great." She slipped inside her car, started it and then waited for Jeff to back up so she could follow him. Her stomach twisted into one big knot. Did she really plan on spending the entire night in his home with him? How did she really feel about it? Nervous, that's how.

Her palms were slick with sweat. It had been a long time since she'd spent an entire night with a man except for Jeff. The one night he'd slept in at her cabin really didn't count or did it? Once he found out her real purpose for being here, he'd cut all ties.

His trust would be gone.

She frowned. Trust. A tricky emotion. One she hoped she didn't lose with this family, but it seemed inevitable.

They turned down a gravel road to the left outside of the main gate of Thunder Ridge. A couple of turns later revealed a beautiful little cabin set back against the hillside. The roughhewn outside reminded her of the rustic cabins of old. You could find them in the mountains of the eastern states and sometimes on the western plains. She loved it on sight. Two windows graced the front. A small porch lined the face of the house, holding two rocking chairs waiting for someone to enjoy the evening while they sipped sweet tea. Maybe someday she'd enjoy the sight with him.

Get those thoughts right out of your head!

"I don't need to be thinking of anything permanent here. He's made it clear he doesn't do long term and I'm not inclined to either."

Seconds later, Ben struggled to open the door of her car for her. So sweet.

Jeff laughed and opened the door for him. "Come on, Ms. Terri. I want to show you my room."

"All right, little man. One second. Let me grab my things." She picked up her purse from the seat and stepped out of the car. Ben grabbed her hand and pulled her toward the door.

"Easy, sport. You don't want to hurt her by pullin' too hard."

"Sorry, Ms. Terri."

"It's fine, Ben. You didn't hurt me." She winked at Jeff, earning herself a genuine smile. She liked his smile. He had the hint of a dimple in his left cheek she hadn't noticed before.

They reached the front porch as Jeff opened the door. "My lady."

"What a grand invitation, sir."

"I hope you enjoy your stay."

"I'm sure I will." The inside of the cabin took her breath away. The rusticity of the furnishings appealed to her primitive side, bringing to life the old west along with a little bit of Indian culture as well. "Jeff, it's gorgeous."

"Thanks."

"Did your ex have anything to do with the décor?"

"Misha? Hell no. She hated this place."

"I'm glad because I love it. It's very much you."

"Come on, Ms. Terri."

Ben pulled her along down the hall. His bedroom had the rustic feel too, but still showed the little boy with his Toy Story bed, a hand carved toy box in the corner and a quilt, obviously made with love by his grandmother.

"Did your mom make the quilt?"

"Yeah." Jeff stuffed his hands in his pockets. "She was so thrilled when we found out Ben was a boy, although she wanted a granddaughter. She didn't really care as long as the child came out healthy. He did at nine pounds and ten ounces."

"What a big boy."

Ben mimicked his dad's stance by shoving his hands in the front pockets of his jeans too. "I have a big boy bed."

"You sure do, pumpkin."

"And I wear big boy panties."

"Great job!" She smiled at Jeff. "I bet he's a handful sometimes."

"Oh yeah. You can say that again."

"See my toys?" Ben pointed to the toy box before he rushed over to lift the lid. "I like Toy Story."

"I can see that." She got down on the floor in front of the toy box. "Who is your favorite?"

"Woody. He's a cowboy like me."

"He sure is." Terri felt her heart overflow with love for this little boy. He had a great dad, awesome grandparents and the affection of his uncles, but he didn't have the love of his mother. It didn't seem fair to her.

"Let's watch a movie," Jeff said, taking her hand and helping her to her feet.

"Yay! Toy Story!"

She laughed as she shuffled out of the room behind Ben and Jeff. "Why am I not surprised."

"Did you think it would be anything else?"

"No, not really once I saw his bedroom. It's okay. I like Toy Story."

"One, two or three?"

"Wow, I didn't realize there was more than one."

"You are so behind the times, lady."

"Apparently. All I can say for myself is I haven't been around kids very much."

"Hang around for a while. We'll teach you, huh Ben?"

"Yes, Daddy."

"Do you want me to?"

"To what?"

"Stick around?"

Both of his shoulders lifted in a shrug. He wouldn't meet her gaze. "I don't know. I mean, we have fun together. I wouldn't mind getting to know you a little better."

"I thought you didn't do relationships?"

"I don't. It wouldn't have to be a relationship. We could just..."

"What? Sleep together?" She didn't like the way this conversation seemed to be headed. *Friends with benefits?*

"We can talk about this after Ben goes to bed."

Ben pushed the movie into the disc player as he flipped on the remote for the television. *Damn, the kid was smart enough to know how to put his own movies on? Apparently.* He plopped down on the soft right in the middle.

The moment he gave her those puppy dog eyes, she couldn't resist. Each of them took a spot on the couch, one on either side of the little boy.

She'd seen the movie before, but low and behold within thirty minutes Ben was asleep leaning against her side. "He's asleep."

"I told you he'd be out inside of a half an hour." Jeff stood and pick up Ben in his arms. "I'll be right back."

Trepidation twisted her guts. They'd talk now and she wasn't sure she was ready for *the talk.* Maybe she could convince him to have sex first. She unbuttoned her blouse. A glimpse of skin should do it. Jeff was a sexual man. She didn't know how he went as long as he did without sex. The moment they'd been together, the whole room threatened to combust.

"Terri?"

"Yeah?" she called back.

"Can you come in a kiss Ben goodnight? He won't go back to sleep until you do."

"Sure. Be right there." *Damn it.* She rebuttoned her blouse, but left it untucked from her jeans. When she walked into the room, the small beside lamp next to the bed was on. Ben had crawled beneath the sheet. "Hey, buddy."

"Can I have a hug and a kiss goodnight?" He raised his arms for her.

"Sure, Ben." She leaned over and his little arms wrapped around her neck. "Night." She kissed him on the forehead, holding back tears his trust and unconditional love toward her brought. *Leave it to a little boy to bring out the feelings the dad is fostering.* "Sleep well."

"Will you be here tomorrow mornin'?"

"I don't know, Ben. I might be back at my cabin near the main lodge, but I'll see you at breakfast if nothing else."

"Okay. I love you, Ms. Terri."

"I love you too, buddy."

Ben rolled over as she wiped her eyes and stood. He needed the love of a mother so much, it hurt her heart.

Jeff took her hand and let her back out to the couch. They sat down side by side. "Thank you for being there for Ben, but I wish you hadn't lied to him."

"I didn't lie to him."

"You said you loved him when I know you don't."

She spun to face him. "How do you know what's in my heart? I do love that little boy. He's a treasure and I wish I was going to be around to see him grow into a man someday. If he's treated right by the women in his life, he'll grow into a special person."

"All right, I don't know how you feel about him, but I don't want him led on either. You know you aren't a permanent part of his life."

"I know that too, Jeff, but I can't help but love him. He's a special little boy."

Jeff ran his hands over his eyes in a weary motion, shoving his hat from his head to let it drop on the arm of the couch. She didn't know how to help him.

Comforting him seemed natural to her. She brought him down so his head lay on her lap. "You've done a great job with him," she said, running her fingers through his hair. "He's a great kid."

"Thanks. I wish his mother loved him as much as I do or you." He glanced up as she pushed his hair off his forehead. "I don't deserve you."

"Sure you do."

"No, I don't. You've been everything a man could want in a woman."

"But?"

"I can't give you my heart like you deserve. I have nothing left to give."

"It doesn't matter, Jeff. We'll go with what we have. Great sex, a kind of friendship or at least that's what I hope we have."

"Yeah."

He grabbed the back of her head and pulled her down to meet his lips. The kiss took her breath away. Everything about the sexy man had her body standing at attention and her panties wet.

"I want you," he whispered against her lips.

"Good. I want you too."

He sat up and spun around. Quick as lightning, he had her on her back as he hovered over her.

"Here?"

"Why not?"

"What about Ben?"

"He won't wake up."

"I'd rather not be caught with my pants down around my ankles by your three-year-old son."

He kissed her, leaving her panting for more. "Let's go into the bedroom. I wanna fuck you hard."

"Oh yeah."

He helped her to her feet, and then lifted her into his arms to carry her down the hall to his bedroom. "You're going to hurt your back, doing this."

"Please. I wrestle cattle, throw hay bales and lifted fifty pound feed sacks two at a time all day long. I can lift one little hundred and twenty pound woman like you."

"God, I wish I weighed a hundred and twenty pounds."

He laughed. "I'm not gonna ask how much you really weigh then."

"A hundred and fifty."

"Wow. Those thirty pounds will kill me!"

He acted like he stumbled under her weight. The jerk. The minute he dropped her in the middle of his bed, she scrambled up to a sitting position. He shut the door and locked it. "Come here."

"No."

"I said, come here."

"I said, no."

He growled low in his throat. The deep rumbling sound sent shivers down her back. Her panties were soaked from his manhandling.

"You're gonna pay for that."

"Oh?"

"I'm gonna have to punish you."

"Say what?"

"Ever been spanked before?" he asked, stalking toward her like a cat on the prowl and she was the prey.

"You aren't going to spank me like a child." Her pussy clenched at the thought. *What the hell? I want him to spank me?*

He quickly flipped her over onto her stomach, dragged her across his legs and proceeded to spank her ass. She screamed.

"*Shh.* You'll do what I tell you while you're with me."

His hand came down hard on her left cheek, then her right.

"If I want you to suck my cock, you will without question." *Smack.* "If I tell you to take your clothes off, you'll do it immediately." *Smack.*

"All right. I will." She sniffed back tears she hadn't realized she'd been shedding.

He rubbed her sore cheeks, until she realized the fire in her butt had spread heat to her pussy.

"I must be crazy to want this, but it's making me hot."

"Ever heard of BDSM?" he asked, helping her to a sitting position.

"Some. I've read some books with it in it."

"I'm not full into it, but I do like to be in control."

"Obviously." She rubbed her butt now that he let her sit up.

"Take your clothes off. Your answer?"

"Yes, Sir?"

"Good girl. You'll learn my wants and needs aren't very particular. I'm not into whips, floggers and the like, but I might want to tie you up sometimes."

"And do what exactly?"

"Eat you out until you are so wet I could ride your ass with just the juices from your pussy."

She'd never had a man there, but she like the sound of having him eat her out. She liked when a man did some of those things to her. Not that she'd had a lot of men in her past, but it sounded good. The few romance novels she'd read with BDSM in turned her inside out. She just wished she knew where this was going. They couldn't have much of a relationship with her living in Houston and his life being all about the ranch. It's a drivable distance, but not convenient for last minute sex.

"I said take off your clothes."

She stood, unbuttoned her shirt and let it fall to the floor behind her. The bra came next. She wanted to be sexy for him, but she felt inadequate and fat. After she unhooked her bra, she let the straps slid down her arms, but held it to her breasts.

"I want to see."

"But I have stretch marks."

"Why?"

"I weighed a lot more a few years ago. I topped the scale at over two hundred pounds. My skin stretched to accommodate."

"I love how you look. I'm not into skinny woman. You've got curves. I love curves on my women."

"Am I your woman?"

"For now, yes."

"I guess it's all I can hope for, huh?"

"You know where I stand on this, Terri. We've talked about it."

"I know. A girl can wish, right?"

"Don't fall in love with me. I don't want to break your heart."

Too late. She sniffed back the burning of tears. *I already do.*

Chapter Ten

The moment she stood naked in front of him, she heard him take in a ragged breath.

"Damn, you're beautiful."

"Thanks."

"I mean it." He stood so he could move closer. With his palms, he cupped both of her breasts in his hands as if he wanted to cherish them. He stepped closer and took one turgid nipple into his mouth.

A soft moan broke from her mouth at the suction of his lips. *God, I love when he sucks my nipples.* She threaded her fingers into his hair, pulling his mouth closer still. His fingers rolled her other nipple while he sucked the first one until her clit throbbed with the beat of her heart. When his hand left her breast to trail down her stomach, she brought her bottom lip between her teeth and bit down to keep from screaming *touch me.* She spread her thighs. His fingers slipped over her mound and between her legs. She whimpered in need.

The tip of his finger grazed over her clit, tearing a tortured groan from her lips. "Yes."

"On your back on the bed."

Her legs wobbled as she moved to comply. She wanted this…wanted him. "You do have condoms, right?"

"As in more than one, yep."

"Thank God." She lay full out on the bed with her head near the top. She didn't bother to remove the covers.

He laughed. "Greedy wench."

"You bet when it comes to you."

"I'm glad. I'm feelin' kind of greedy myself tonight."

"Can I suck you?"

"Not now. We need to take the edge off first. I'm about to blow. I probably will the moment I get inside your hot little pussy."

"I need you, Jeff. Please."

"I need to do somethin' first, darlin'. I want to taste you."

She spread her thighs as he moved to settle himself between them. The first swipe of his tongue had her hips coming up off the bed.

"Easy, darlin'."

"God, Jeff."

Her pussy felt on fire. She wanted him to hurry, but on the other hand, she needed him to take his time. She wanted to come. Not too fast, not too slow. It was torture, pure unadulterated torture.

Within seconds, she felt heat crawl up her legs and explode in her pelvis, tearing a muffled scream from her throat.

"Nice save, babe."

Sweat beaded on her upper lip. *Yeah, that's sexy.*

He moved over her and took her mouth with his in a deep, penetrating kiss.

"You still have your clothes on," she murmured when they broke apart for air.

"I sure do. Now I want you to undress me."

"Can I lick and touch?"

"All you want, darlin'." He stood up in the middle of the room with his hands at his sides, just waiting.

She got to her feet and stopped in front of him to admire the view. His wide chest tapered to trim hips. He always seemed so cleaned and pressed when she saw him. With all of the work he did on the ranch, he never seemed to have a hair out of place. She wanted to ruffle him up.

She let her lips skim over his jawline as her hands unbuttoned each button on the front of his shirt, very slowly. When she reached the bottom, she pulled the material from the waistband of his jeans, letting it flutter to a rest at his waist. "I love how you taste."

He groaned and she smiled against his skin. Torture would be sweet tonight.

The five o'clock shadow of a beard on his jaw tickled her tongue as she ran it over his skin.

He lifted his hands to touch her, but she swatted them away. "No touching. It's my turn." They dropped back to his sides, but he clenched his hands into fists.

With the shirt loose, she pushed it off his shoulders to reveal the breadth of his chest. No doubt about it, the man was built. Hefting hay all day sure built muscles upon muscles on his gorgeous chest. His arms bulged when she ran her hands down his biceps to push the shirt to the floor. "I love your chest."

She reached for his belt buckle, fully aware of the ridged cock beneath her fingers. She ran her fingernail down the outside of his jeans over his cock, dragging another groan from his lips.

"You're gonna pay for torturing me, darlin'."

She loved when he called her that. It made her feel special…his.

"Oh, I think you love it, cowboy."

"I do, but you're killin' me."

When she had his pants undone, she pushed them as well as his boxer briefs to the floor at his feet. He'd kicked off his boots while they'd watched the movie with Ben, so they didn't have those to deter them now.

He stepped out of his clothes, pushing them to the side with his foot. She loved him with her hands and her mouth, licking, sucking and trailing her lips from his ear, over his collarbone to his nipples. The ridged tips called to her. She flicked them with her tongue, bringing them to hard points of flesh.

Her next move was to drop to her knees and run her tongue from his balls to the tip of his cock.

"Just your mouth. No hands."

She put her hands behind her back, determined to suck him until he exploded in her mouth. The head of his cock was soft. The whole thing was soft skin over hardened steel. She couldn't believe he'd had the entire length inside her more than once. The man wasn't small by any means.

With as much finesse as she could without the use of her hands, she ran her tongue around the head, up and down his shaft, licked his balls and literally made love to his cock with her mouth.

"Enough."

She shook her head as she sucked hard.

"I'm gonna come in your mouth then."

She nodded quickly running her tongue around the head again before she sucked the majority of his length into her mouth.

"Fuck!"

The warm, salty taste of his cum wasn't unpleasant as it shot to the back of her throat. She swallowed every bit until his legs wobbled and he pulled himself from her mouth to collapse on the bed.

"You didn't have to do that, darlin'."

"I wanted to."

"Thank you," he said, taking her face between his hands and kissing her. "Give me a minute to recuperate and I'll take care of you again."

"Take care of both of us."

"Yeah."

She sat next to him on the bed before she scooted up to rest against the headboard. He followed her up to sit next to her, pulling her against his chest. He kissed her on the forehead much like she'd done with Ben.

Did he care for her at all? She wasn't sure. Sometimes he seemed to let her in and then he'd shut himself off from her like he was afraid to care. He said he didn't have a heart left to give anyone. He was wrong. She just knew he had it in him to love someone, she wasn't sure it would be her though, especially when he found out what she'd done after she talked to Jeremiah.

* * * *

It didn't take any time at all for him to be hard again. He had it so bad for her. Sex though, it was only sex. He couldn't think of anything else. Going beyond that wasn't an option. Not now, not ever.

"Ready so fast, cowboy?"

"You bet, city girl."

"I told you, I'm not a city girl."

"Honey, from the minute I saw you, your clothes screamed city girl from the tips of your brand new boots to those designer jeans."

She laughed. "I was tryin' to blend in."

"Not like that you weren't."

"Not so much, eh?"

"Do you even own any other boots?"

"No."

"You would have blended in better if you would have worn your power suit."

"Power suit?"

"I assume you own one." He glanced down at her confused face. "You know, tight skirt, white silk blouse, blazer jacket, and fuck me pumps."

She sputtered in indignation.

"You do have one."

"Of course, I do, but I don't call it my power suit."

"I'd like to see you in only those shoes." He moved sideways and slid down in the bed, taking her with him. "I want to be inside you."

"You need a condom first."

"No problem, darlin'." He reached over to the nightstand, grabbed a condom and rolled it on in two seconds flat. "Ready for me?"

"More than ready."

He moved between her legs, rubbing the head of his cock on her clit.

"Wait."

"Wait? Why?"

"I want to do something." He moved off her and stood on the side of the bed. "Come with me." He held out his hand until she got to her feet. Once she was standing beside him, he lifted her so she had to wrap her legs around his hips. With his cock poised at her pussy, he waited for the perfect moment to slide home. He moved so her back was against the wall. "Now, this is fuckin' awesome."

"Oh shit," she growled low in her throat as he pushed his cock into her hot pussy. "Oh, God!"

He pulled her legs up so they lay across his forearms, giving him more leverage and deeper penetration. It was his turn for his eyes to roll in the back of his head. The heat of her pussy beckoned with each thrust. He could feel each scrape of her G spot along the head of his cock, dragging every moan from his mouth. He wouldn't last long like this. Each stroke of his cock threatened to end their erotic dance too quickly. He wanted this to last, wanted to bring her along for the ride.

"You need to come, darlin'."

"I can't. I need a little more..." Her words trailed off into a moan.

He pistoned his hips in sharp, jabbing thrusts, bringing them both to the brink in seconds. "Come with me."

Her high scream was smothered by his mouth as they both came apart together.

His legs wobbled, unable to hold them. He released her legs, pulled out his cock, and let her slide down his body so they could both catch their breath without falling down into a heap of melted bone and muscle on the floor. He'd never come so hard in his life.

They stumbled back to the bed, collapsing on the coverlet in a heap. "Wow."

"Yeah, you can say that again."

"Wow."

She laughed and shook her head. "You're impossible."

"But, wow."

"I get it."

They laughed together for a moment before he disposed of the condom in a trashcan near the bed. "Do you want to watch a movie for a while?"

"Sure. What kind of movies do you have besides Toy Story?"

"Some action flicks and maybe a few chick flicks too."

"Can I pick?"

He pulled her down on the bed with him. "Sure, but let's lie here for a bit before we rush off to watch a movie." He ran his fingers down her arm. "I kind of like having you here next to me."

"Do you want me to stay until morning?"

"If you want to. I won't push, but I enjoyed waking up next to you the other day even if it wasn't planned."

"As you exploded in a panic that your family would find out about us sleeping together and have a cow."

"You don't understand. We have a rule about sleeping with the guests. I can't very well enforce it if I'm doin' it."

"I think it's a silly rule."

"You would." He wet his finger before rubbing it around her nipple.

Goose bumps rose on her chest as her nipple hardened into a small nub. "You keep that up and we won't be watching any movie, at least not for a little while yet."

He palmed her breast. "Fine by me. I like fuckin' you."

"I got that impression, yes, which is a good thing since I like it too."

Concern crossed his mind. He needed to ask her some questions. Her information digging had both him and his dad troubled. "We need to talk."

The look on her face told him she was confused again. "Uh-oh. About what?"

"Why are you askin' so many questions about the ranch?"

"I told you. I'm curious."

"Curious doesn't explain wanting to know the financial stuff. Curious might describe wanting to know what kind of horses we have."

"It's nothing, Jeff."

"I don't know whether to trust you or not."

She bit her lip. A sure sign of nervousness. "You're sleeping with me, but you don't trust me?"

"You do work for the enemy."

"Only in the sense that I'm gathering information for them on the area."

"Are you sure you aren't giving them any other information on us?" She glanced away. "Terri?"

"I haven't told them anything."

"Why does it sound like there's a *but* in there?"

"No but." She rolled away from him and sat up on the side of the bed. "I thought we were going to watch a movie."

"I thought we were gonna make love...I mean have sex again?" *Great, dumbass! What a stupid thing to say.*

Fluffing her hair with her fingers gave away more of her nervousness. Why did she seem upset by the questioning? *Damn it. I should never have started this.*

He rolled off the side of the bed and grabbed his pants. One foot in, then the other. He needed to keep his mind off where his thoughts were headed right now. Trust came hard for him and right now she wasn't doing anything to cement his trust in her. "Terri?"

"I can't talk about it, Jeff. Please don't ask me to."

"You've told me you were gathering information on the area. Like what?" he asked, sitting down on the side of the bed next to her.

One of his old T-shirts now graced her shoulders, covering up her tempting body. Her scent drifted to his nose from her hair. *Damn, she smells good.*

"Information on the soil, water, those kinds of things. Nothing special."

"What does our financial stuff have to do with that?"

She jumped to her feet. "Nothing. All right. I was curious. That's it!"

"I don't believe you."

"No shit!"

She threw off his T-shirt and pulled her clothes on.

"Where are you goin'?"

"Back to my cabin. Obviously you don't trust me and you don't believe me. I can't be with a man who thinks I'm totally up to no good."

"If you aren't up to something, why are you so defensive?" he asked, coming to his feet too. Something wasn't right here.

"Fine. I'm telling them every fucking thing I can find out about your family. Your financial situation, everything!"

"Why?"

"Because they want to buy you out!" She pushed her fingers through her hair. "Hell if I know, Jeff. I'm an architect. I'm not a damn financial wizard. They want information on you. I've been gathering it, but I'm not sure I'm giving it to them."

"You're plannin' on betraying my family?"

"I'm not planning anything. Some of the things I've found on the area lead me to believe things aren't as they seem."

Anger zipped through him. "I think you need to leave."

"I am!" She shoved her feet back into the shoes she'd worn to the house.

"Leave my family alone. I want you off the ranch tomorrow morning."

"I'll leave when I'm damned good and ready."

"You aren't welcome here anymore."

"I have a job to do."

"Do it from someone else's ranch."

"Fuck you! I'll do what I need to do. Plus, I've paid for the time to stay here. If you don't like it, too bad. Talk to your mother."

"I will!"

She stomped out to the living room, grabbing her purse from the couch on her way by.

The door slammed on her way out and he raked his fingers through his hair. *What the hell just happened?*

His cell phone jingled on the counter where he'd left his keys. "What?"

"Tell your family their done in the Hill Country."

The phone clicked in his ear.

"Great. Now I'm getting threatening phone calls too? Jesus."

He grabbed a beer from the refrigerator and down half of it in several long gulps. Trust. *Damn, it's a two edge sword.* He learned not to trust a woman when Misha stabbed him in the back. Now Terri. He'd really begun to think she was different than any other woman he'd known, but apparently not. She used him to get close to his family, just like Misha.

What the fuck? Why do I keep running into these bitches out to use the hell out of me?

Chapter Eleven

Terri walked into the diner in town through the tinkling glass door. The '50s décor was a welcome change after everything cowboy the last few days. The checkered tablecloths gracing each of the tables with vinyl and metal chairs at each one seemed almost quaint.

After she'd left Jeff the night before, she'd received a phone call from the partners demanding to meet her today. Up until now, she hadn't decided whether she was going to give them the information she'd gathered or not.

She took a seat in one of the booths. The vinyl seat felt cool against her back and legs.

"Hi there, sweetie. What can I get you to drink?"

"Coffee, please, Ann."

"Coming right up." Ann stayed for a minute as she tilted her head to the side. "Where's Jeff?"

Terri frowned. "Working I guess. I really don't know."

"Oh, I'm sorry. I thought you two were friends from what Nina told me."

"We were, but things have changed a bit with our friendship. He doesn't want to see me anymore."

"Now, that seems just like Jeffery. Stupid cuss."

"Can I get that coffee, please?"

"Oh sure, honey. Sorry." Ann shuffled off but came back a moment later with the coffee pot and a mug. "Do ya need cream?"

"Yes, please."

"What would you like to eat?"

"Just coffee for now. I'm meeting someone."

Ann nodded. "Okay. Just holler when you're ready."

"Thank you."

When Ann had walked away, Terri looked at the door to the diner with trepidation. She didn't want to do this anymore. Betraying Jeff and his family left a bad taste in her mouth, but what else was she supposed to do? If she told the developers the truth, they'd try to buy out the entire Hill Country. The information she gleaned from her research told her the piece of property next to Thunder Ridge would make a fine development property but if they tried to put in a golf course or something along those lines, they would have to divert a lot of the natural springs to keep the thing watered. She knew a course was part of the developers plan for their property.

One more thing she'd learned. Jeff's family had never had their property tested for oil. The soil samples she'd taken initially told her there was a possibility. She wanted to tell Jeff. She wanted his family to drill and see if there might be a rich oil deposit on their property, but he wouldn't talk to her now. Not after their blowup the night before.

"Terri?"

"Yes? Hi, Mr. Cole."

He held out his hand for her to shake.

"Hello," she said taking his hand. The sweaty palm grossed her out, making her shiver in revulsion.

"May I?"

"Of course."

Ann appeared seconds later. "Coffee?"

"Yes, please."

As soon as Ann departed again, she turned to the gentleman at the table with her. "I don't know why you wanted to meet this morning."

"We need a report."

"There's nothing to tell you other than the information I have on the area with the soil, water, etcetera."

"What about information on the family?"

"I don't have anything."

"Nothing? Surely you gleaned something from your time spent with the eldest son?"

"No."

"You mean you were fuck buddies with him and didn't learn anything?"

"Excuse me?"

"We know you've been getting cozy with Jeffery Young. Surely you gained some kind of information we can use?"

"The Young family is a stable part of this community. Leave them alone."

"We want that property, Terri, and you're going to help us get it."

"I'm not doing any such thing."

He tapped the spoon on the edge of the cup, grating on her nerves like fingernails on a chalkboard.

"Then the loan you took out to open your business comes due immediately."

"You can't do that! That's a quarter of a million dollar loan. I don't have that kind of money."

"I'm sorry, but it's your choice. Tell me what you know or the loan comes due today."

"There's nothing to tell."

"I find that hard to believe, my dear."

She shivered. The blackness of the man's eyes made her think of the devil, all he needed was a couple horns sprouting from his forehead. These men were cutthroat and now she was in their sights.

"I don't know anything. They've been very closed mouth about their family and their business. They haven't told me a single thing that would be helpful to you."

"Let us be the judge of that."

She inhaled sharply. What the hell could she tell him to get him to leave her and Jeff's family alone? "They are very stable financially. They haven't been sued for any accidents or anything on their property. The cattle and the guests keep them in a good position." She bit her lips. "There is something."

"What?"

"Some information I found out about the property itself. You can't build on it."

"What?" He slapped his hand down on the table, making her jump. "That's crazy. We've got plans. We've got investors. You're wrong!"

"I'm not wrong. Water rights are held by the Young family for the property you want to build on. All of the natural springs run through their property."

"We'll ruin them so they'll have to sell."

Think quickly.

"I've also checked with the local zoning codes. The area isn't zoned for a development."

"We've already talked to the zoning committee about changing the zoning."

His self-righteous smirk made her want to slap it off his lips.

Her cell phone buzzed. "I need to check this." The report she'd been waiting for popped up on her screen. *Thank you God!* "I just received a report I've been waiting for. You can't build on the property you already own because it's a natural habitat for a rare bird. It's now been classified as a wildlife refuge."

"No fucking way."

"Yes, way." She turned the cell around so he could see it. "I spotted the bird when I was out riding with my 'fuck buddy' as you called him. I wasn't sure until now."

"We'll move the damned bird."

"You can't. The paperwork is being processed as we speak to reclassify the property. There's nothing you can do to stop it."

He jumped to his feet, pointing one finger at her. "You've done this!"

She raised an eyebrow, but managed not to grin.

"You're going to be ruined. I'll see to it myself."

"Do your best. I didn't do anything wrong. I'm just doing my job, but you know what? If it means keeping you from ruining a nice family's livelihood and kicking them off property that has been in their family for a long time, then so be it."

Ann stepped to the side of the table. "You need to leave, sir. Your coffee is on the house."

"You can't kick me out of this establishment."

"Oh, yes I can. I own this diner and I don't want your kind here. Good day, sir."

Mr. Cole sputtered a few obscenities under his breath, grabbed his briefcase from the bench and then stomped like a two year old throwing a tantrum as he left the diner.

"Thank you, Ann."

"You're welcome, honey." She slid into the booth seat. "Tell me what's going on between you and my nephew?"

"Nothing really."

"I think there is."

She ran her finger around the rim of her coffee cup as she stared at the brown liquid hoping for some answers. "It doesn't matter."

Ann patted her hand. "What you've done for the family matters. You can bet Nina and James will hear of this because I'll be sure to tell them."

She focused on the friendly face of the waitress across from her. "Please don't. I didn't do anything."

"Yes, you did. You saved their place from those vultures. They have the money and the resources to close Thunder Ridge should they decide to."

Her heart rate slowed now since Mr. Cole had left, leaving her feeling relieved but anxious at the same time. Would he come back? Would they be able to change the mind of the wildlife committee with enough money greasing palms? She hoped not, but this might not be over yet. "Luck was on their side. If I hadn't spotted the bird, things would have not gone as well."

"I heard what you said to him. You were trying to stall hoping for this news from the wildlife people, weren't you?"

"Yes. I tried everything I could come up with to make him think they wouldn't be able to build on the property. I knew the report would come through this morning, but I didn't know when."

"God watches out for us in mysterious ways at times."

"Yes, he does."

Ann's gaze narrowed. "What did you and Jeffery fight over?"

"All of this." She waved her hand indicating the entire situation. "He knew I worked for the developers and that I was asking a lot of questions. I needed the information from his family. Originally, the developers wanted me to find out something to ruin them, but I couldn't do it. Never mind my feelings for Jeff. I just couldn't see doing anything to hurt such nice people." She took a sip of her coffee, now gone cold. "I hate cold coffee."

"Let me warm it up for you." Ann took the cup and returned a moment later with a fresh one.

"Thank you."

"Now, go on."

"Nina, James…everyone has been so nice to me. Even Jeremiah gave me the information I needed to be able to bluff Mr. Cole with until the report came through, but I couldn't tell Jeff what I was up to. He thinks I got the information to give to the developers."

"Which he was correct in a way."

"True, but I couldn't tell him the real reason behind my need for the information. I wasn't sure the wildlife committee would come through."

"So tell him now."

"He won't talk to me." She sipped her coffee. "Besides, he doesn't trust me now."

"His ex-wife took care of the trust thing."

"Yes, she did."

Ann tapped her fingers on her lips. "I think he'll come around when he finds out what you've done."

"It doesn't matter. I'm going home to Houston today. My work here is done. I have to make sure Mr. Cole's threat is nothing more than a threat. He could kill my business if he forces those I borrowed the funds to start my business from into making my loan come due. I don't have a quarter of a million dollars to pay them off."

"Don't worry, honey. Everythin' will work itself out."

She squeezed Ann's hand. "Thank you for listening. I think I'll take breakfast now."

"Good. What can I get you?"

After she ordered a ham and cheese omelet, she sat back in the booth with a satisfied smile on her face. She'd done a good deed. It felt wonderful to her heart even as the organ broke inside her chest. Somehow during the time on the ranch, she'd come to care for the enigma of a man who wouldn't open his heart to her no matter how much she tried or what she said. He wouldn't trust her now because of her deceit.

As the bell dinged over the door, she glanced up. Nina Young strolled in and took a seat across from her.

"What's this I hear you're leaving for home today? You still have a good few days left at the ranch."

"Hello to you too, Nina." She laughed.

"I'm not into niceties when my eldest son's heart is involved."

Terri shook her head and glanced over at Ann. "She works fast."

"Yes, she does. Good thing I was already in town at the bank and courthouse dealing with Jeff's ex this morning when she called."

Ann placed a cup of coffee in front of Nina and Terri's plate in front of her. The food look fabulous as her stomach rumbled in earnest.

"Go ahead and eat while we talk."

"You mean while you talk?"

"Yes." Nina smiled. "I like you, Terri. I like what you do for Jeff. He needs someone like you in his life."

"He doesn't want me in his life. He's told me as much."

"He doesn't know what he needs or wants."

"And you do?"

"Yes. Ann told me what you did for us. I want to tell Jeff."

"Please don't."

"He needs to know he can trust you. You saved our ranch."

"He can't trust me. He knew all along what I was doing and he chose to believe the worst in me...in all women."

"Damn his ex-wife."

"She did a number on him, yes, but it doesn't explain everything."

"You've heard she left him on their wedding night to party with her friends and didn't return for two days?"

Terri nodded as she took another bite of her omelet.

"Well the part most people don't know except me and his father is that he found her with another man."

"Seriously?"

"Two days into their marriage, she cheated on him. In fact, at first we didn't know whether Ben was Jeff's or someone else's. Why he didn't leave her ass the minute he caught her cheating, I don't know except he was in love with her."

"He's a lot more patient and loving than any man I've known."

"You know he loves you, right?"

Her stomach flipped over. "No he doesn't."

"He's been nothing but a bear this morning. Slamming things. Cussing up a storm. When I asked him what was wrong, he told me you were gone and you weren't coming back." She shook her head. "The sadness in his eyes tore at my heart. Yes, he's angry because he feels like you betrayed him and us, but we both know you didn't. He needs to know the details of what happened so he can realize his feelings for you are genuine."

"I don't want him to know."

"You don't care about him?"

"I care too much for him."

"I don't think anyone can care too much."

Terri shook her head and glanced down at her plate. "Please, Nina. Let it go."

"All right. I will because you've asked me to, but I think you're making a big mistake."

"It wouldn't be the first time." She finished her meal and pushed the plate out of the way. "I'll be leaving for home in a couple of hours. I'll be back to the ranch to get my stuff."

"I wish you would talk to Jeff."

"I know, but it's not meant to be."

The bell tinkled as another couple came in. "Hey, Ma!"

"Oh my. I didn't realize you two were coming back today!" Nina stood and hugged them both before she turned around to face Terri again. "Terri, this is my son Joel and his new bride Mesa. They just returned from their honeymoon."

"It's nice to meet you." She noticed immediately the blue eyes and identical features to Jason and Joshua. "So you're the third in the triplets."

"Yeah." Joel laughed before he put his arm around the cute woman next to him. The love they shared shone bright in both their gazes.

"I've met everyone on the ranch but you."

"You're staying on the ranch?"

"Only until this afternoon. I'm headed home to Houston."

"Too bad. I would have like to get to know you," Mesa added.

Ann walked up and kissed both of them on the cheek. "Aren't they so cute together?"

"Stop, Ann." The crimson coloring staining Joel's cheeks made Terri laugh.

"I'm trying to convince her to stay longer. She's been seeing Jeff."

"What?" Joel's face registered his shock with wide eyes and an open mouth. "Jeff? I didn't think he liked women anymore."

"Well he likes Terri or did until last night. They had a fight."

"It wasn't really a fight, Nina."

"A misunderstanding then."

"You should stick around and try to work things out," Mesa said. "He's really not a bad guy once you get to know him."

"I think she knows him pretty well."

"Ah." Mesa smiled a knowing little grin.

Heat rose in Terri's cheeks.

"Well, we're heading home." Joel took Mesa's hand. "We just happened to see the ranch truck here on our way back from the airport."

"I'll see you at home then." Nina stood and grabbed Terri's check as Mesa and Joel waved goodbye. "Breakfast is on me."

"No, it's not. I've got it."

"Nonsense. I ruined your breakfast with talk so I'll pay for it. Ann, is that her total?" She shoved a twenty dollar bill at Ann along with the ticket.

"Thank you. You really didn't have to buy my meal."

"It's the least I can do. I'll see you back at the ranch too." She hugged Terri. "Think about what I said, honey. He does love you and I think you love him too, but you two have some talking to do."

"I will."

Nina left with a wave of her hand as the bell tinkled on the door.

Terri felt lost. She'd become such a part of the family and life on the ranch in the several days she'd spent there, she didn't want to leave. She finished her coffee and stood. No time like the present. Getting her stuff and hitting the road sounded like a great idea, although the possibility of running into Jeff soured her stomach. She didn't want to deal with him and the hateful looks he'd be giving her, but it wasn't to be helped. Hopefully he'd be busy and wouldn't even know she'd been there and gone.

"Thanks for everything, Ann. You've been a great help."

"You're welcome, sweetie. I hope you and Jeff work things out."

"I don't think we will, but thank you for the sentiment."

Terri grabbed her purse and headed for the door. *Might as well get this over with.*

Chapter Twelve

Terri inhaled on a sigh as she drove through the gate of the ranch. Longhorns grazed in the distance to the left in the open area. Birds flocked from one of the juniper trees as she drove by, clouding the sky with their mass. Gravel crunched under the tires of her car. The sunlight filtered through the puffy white clouds overhead. The main lodge house came into view along with the small cabins to the right, which included hers. Her little home away from home. She closed her eyes for a moment hoping the burn of tears would go away before she had to face packing her stuff for the trip back to Houston. The big city didn't feel like home anymore. The slow pace of life here on the ranch felt more like family than anything she'd ever experienced.

When she opened her eyes she caught movement by the barn. A cowboy stood leaning against the doorframe with his arms crossed over his chest and a black cowboy hat shading his eyes. Jeff. *Damn.* She'd really hoped she wouldn't see him, but it was almost as if he'd been waiting for her to show up, watching for her car or something.

The ache in her chest made her rub the spot over her sternum. She hoped she wasn't having a heart attack or something. *Yeah, more like heartache.*

He didn't move. Just stood there watching with lips firmed in a straight line. She couldn't see his eyes, but the slash of his lips told her he wasn't happy.

She stepped from her car, slamming the door behind her firmly. This wouldn't take long, she hoped, and she'd be on her way back to her life.

With her back ramrod straight, she headed for the front of the cabin, keeping an eye on the man in her peripheral vision. He never moved. She couldn't even tell if he blinked. The concentration on his face never changed.

She opened the door to her cabin to glance inside. Nothing had changed. Her clothes still hung in the small closet. Her suitcase still sat open on the dresser waiting for her to put her clothes in it. Her computer sat on the desk right where she'd left it when she'd sent the report off to the wildlife committee the day before.

Jeff had changed her life irrevocably, but still life went on. How she would move on without him, she wasn't sure, but she had to. He didn't want her. The trust was gone and if she learned one thing about Jeffery Young, when you lost his trust, you lost everything.

She exhaled sharply as she shut the door. Tears formed, burning her eyelids as they trickled down her face. She would miss this place. Maybe someday she would come back for a visit, but then again no. Seeing him again would tear out her heart.

A knock sounded on the door. Did she dare answer it? Jeff? She hoped not. She didn't think she could face him right now. She bit her lip as the knock sounded again.

"I know you're in there, Terri. Open the door."

It was him.

"Leave me alone, Jeff. Haven't you done enough?"

"I want to talk to you."

"You made it perfectly clear we were done last night."

"Open the door or I'll bust it down."

"Fine." She grumbled under her breath about stubborn-ass men as she opened the door. *Damn it.* He looked almost good enough to eat in his cowboy finery. He made even dirty boots and jeans look damn good. "What do you want?"

He pushed his way inside the room and closed the door. "You're leaving?"

She looked at him like he'd lost his mind. "Of course, I'm leaving. You told me to. My work here is done. The developers got their report."

"And?"

"And what?"

"What are they planning to do with it?"

Apparently Nina hadn't told him...yet. Terri paced the room, hoping for something, but she didn't know what. Did he want her to stay? Did he really love her like Nina suggested? His words sounded clipped and fraught with anger. "I don't know. They weren't happy with my results. I'm sure they plan on getting another opinion, but it won't matter. Things won't change."

"What did you tell them?"

"I can't divulge my findings."

"So this is it?"

"This is what, Jeff? What are you asking me? Last night you said you wanted me gone. I'm going. What else is there?"

"Nothin' I guess."

"Exactly. There's nothing between us. There's nothing left to say."

"I guess this is goodbye then."

"Yeah." She wiped her face, not realizing tears still streaked her cheeks until his eyes narrowed. "Tell Ben goodbye for me."

"I will."

"He's a great kid, Jeff. Take care of him."

"I will."

"I hope things work out with Misha. It would be great if she would disappear from his life, but I have a feeling you'll be dealing with her for the rest of yours."

"You didn't hear?"

"Hear what?"

"The paramedics found her dead in her house this morning. The initial diagnosis was cardiac arrest from overdose."

"Wow, really?"

"Yeah. I haven't told Ben yet. I'm not sure how to tell him."

"Just be up front with him. I'm sure he'll miss her."

"Yeah. I never wished her dead even though she was a pain in my ass."

Terri stepped toward him and wrapped her arms around his neck. She needed to feel his heat one more time before she walked out of his life forever. Jeff returned the hug. They stood that way for several minutes as she fought the return of her tears. "Give him a hug for me," she whispered.

"I will."

She closed her eyes and inhaled his scent. Musk, man and horse. She'd never be able to be around livestock again without thinking of him. "I guess this is goodbye."

"Yeah, I guess so."

She stepped out of his arms and said, "Thanks for everything and I hope things work out for the best with the land next door."

"I hope so too."

"Just know I did my best."

He tilted his head to the side with a look of confusion clouding his eyes, but he didn't linger. His boots sounded hollow on the tile floor beneath his feet as he approached the door. With a quick look behind him, he returned the sunglasses to his eyes and disappeared with a soft click of the panel behind him.

* * * *

Jeff watched from the barn as Terri loaded her suitcase into the car. He wouldn't ask her to stay. He couldn't. His trust in her had been broken by the secrets and lies she'd told even though his heart said they didn't matter.

"You're an idiot, son."

"Thanks, Mom."

Nina stood next to him watching Terri slide into her car and shut the door. The car started a few minutes before she backed out and slowly disappeared down the gravel drive. They continued to watch together until her car disappeared from sight.

"Have you told Ben about Misha yet?"

"No. I need to, but I'm not sure how."

"Just tell him the truth, Jeff."

"What is the truth, Mom? She didn't love him. Not like a mother should."

"I wouldn't tell him she overdosed on drugs since we don't exactly know what the cause of death is."

"There's no denying it from what I heard from the paramedics. They found Meth crystals and needles at her apartment. I'm sorry I didn't notice track marks before or the fact that she seemed wired every time I saw her."

"It explains her manic behavior when she showed up here earlier and her demand for money."

"Yeah, it does."

"Jeffery?"

"Yeah, Mom?"

"Why did you let Terri leave?"

"What do you mean?"

"You're in love with her, aren't you?"

He pushed his hat back on his head. "No."

"Yes you are, son. I can see it in your eyes."

"Even through the sunglasses?"

"Jeffery."

"It doesn't matter, Mom. I can't trust her and without trust, there's nothin'."

"Why do you say that?"

"Hello?" He looked at his mom like she had two heads. "How can you ask something like that? After what Misha pulled and knowing Terri was working for the developers while they tried to put us out of business?"

"But in the long run, she didn't, right?"

"I don't know, Mom. We don't know what they're gonna do. They might still succeed with their plans. Terri wouldn't tell me what she told them in her report. It was like she didn't trust me."

"Now there's a turn of the cards. A woman not trust you?"

"You aren't funny."

His mom brushed her fingers from his cheek to his ear like she used to do when he was little. The soothing motion calmed his heart some. He knew he would always have the love of his family to fall back on and now he didn't have to worry about Misha trying to take their son from him ever again. Was it wrong to be glad she was dead? Maybe. He'd have to have a chat with God tonight on his knees to beg for forgiveness.

"Honey, you're in love with her. Why don't you admit it?"

"In love with who?"

"Terri."

"Because it doesn't matter what I feel for her. She betrayed me."

She exhaled through her mouth in a heavy sigh. "I wish I knew what to say to make you see she's the right girl for you."

"She might have been, but we'll never know now." He pulled his hat from his head and raked his fingers through his hair. "I guess I'm destined to live alone."

The lunch bell clanged calling them inside. "We need to talk more after lunch. I have something to tell you I think might make a difference and maybe even make you go after her."

He frowned wondering what his mother might have to tell him. What could possibly change his mind concerning Terri? "Why don't you tell me now?"

Nina patted his cheek with her hand. "Because I want to give the girl a head start and give you the time to come to the same conclusion the rest of the family already has. You're very much in love with her, but you can't see past the hurt in your heart to see the wonderful woman she truly is."

His mother turned to head for the main lodge with him bringing up the rear with slow, steady footsteps. *What am I supposed to think? Obviously Mom knows something Terri's done that might redeem her in my eyes, but I can't possibly think what.*

Lunch would be a noisy affair. The ranch was busy this week with guests. Every cabin had a family or a group in it. *All but Terri's now.*

Jeff detoured toward her cabin. The door was unlocked so he slowly pushed it open. The room smelled like her. Her soft scent enveloped him bringing his thoughts back to the night they'd made love in this room. She'd given herself to him without reservation. Took everything he'd dished out with a relish few women he'd known could. It felt right. She felt right.

His heart lay tattered in pieces in his chest. She'd come and gone taking it with her as she drove down the driveway on her way back to Houston. Did she feel anything for him? He didn't know. Could she? Possibly. She cared for Ben. He was certain of that fact.

Would she give him another chance if he asked? Could he put his heart out there like that again hoping she wouldn't betray him like Misha?

What he wanted from Terri went beyond what he thought he'd felt for Misha. He'd never loved Misha like this.

Terri had his heart in the palm of her hand.

I love her.

The thought brought a smile to his mouth. He loved her. His heart felt lighter than it had in three years.

He spun around and headed for the main lodge. Going after her would be the right thing to do. He would convince her he loved her and wanted her to come back to Thunder Ridge with him if it was the last thing he ever did.

The big heavy door on the side of the building gave way to his insistent push. The crowd grew quiet as he walked toward the family table. An expectancy hung in the air.

"I love her!"

"It's about damned time you figured it out," Jeremiah said with a laugh.

The whole room erupted into cheers.

"I'm glad you understand now, son," Nina said, patting the chair next to her for him to sit. "Eat lunch and then go after her. Bring her back here where she belongs."

Soon the crowd of guests had their fill of food and the family took their places to pile their own plates. Jeff sat down with his and Ben's.

"Daddy, did you ask Terri to be my new mom yet?"

"Not yet, buddy, but soon."

"But she left and didn't say goodbye."

"She told me to kiss you." He leaned over and kissed Ben's head. "And tell you she loved you, but she'd see you again soon."

"Yay!" Ben clapped his hands. "When?"

"Hopefully before the weekend, son."

"I'm glad you've come to your senses, Jeff," James added to the conversation.

"What did you want to tell me, Mom?"

"Terri saved the ranch."

"Huh?"

"She had a meeting with one of developers this morning. Because of the information she gathered, they won't be able to build on their land. It's now a wildlife refuge because of a rare bird she spotted. It's useless to them now."

"She what? Really?"

"Yeah. They won't bother us anymore."

"Why didn't she tell me?"

"Because she didn't want your love based on something she did to save the ranch, I imagine. You needed to come to the conclusion you loved her for herself. If you couldn't, then you didn't love her enough."

He turned to face his mother. He needed to understand some things about women and how they thought. Of course, it was probably too late for that. "So why tell me now?"

"You said you loved her. You've moved past the hurt Misha caused and found love again with someone who will love you with all of her heart."

"What if she doesn't love me? What if I drive all the way to Houston and she slams the door in my face?"

"Do you think that's the truth?"

"I'm not sure. She never said she loved me."

Nina patted his hand. "Son, until you confess your love for her, she'll hold her love inside her heart and only bring it out when she's alone and can cry without worrying about someone wondering what's wrong. Women do those kinds of things."

"I need to go now." He jumped to his feet. "I have to catch her before she gets home."

"Sit down and eat, Jeff. She doesn't have much of a head start on you. Besides," Nina's eyebrow rose over her left eye, "you'll need her address to get to her home, wrap her in your arms and never let her go."

Mom is probably right. She's been right about everything so far. He nodded at his mother, who gave him a sly grin. *I knew I should have paid more attention to her when I had the chance.*

Lunch couldn't be eaten fast enough for him while he contemplated what he would say to Terri when he caught her. Catch her he would whether it be somewhere along the way or once she got home. She'd have a good hour head start on him, but he'd catch her one way or another.

The moment he finished eating, he grabbed his plate and set it in the dirty dish bin. "I'm going now."

"Go get 'er Jeff," Joel said from his spot next to Mesa. "I can vouch for the bein' in love thing."

"Shut up, Joel," Jonathan replied. "You're sappy in love."

"Just wait until he comes back with her. He'll be the same way."

"God, I hope not. Y'all are makin' me ill."

"You'll get your turn, Jonathan. Just wait."

"I need the address."

"Wait a second. I'll be right back." His mom disappeared for a minute before returning with a sticky note. "Here. Be careful."

"Watch Ben, please," Jeff asked his mom.

"Of course, son. We'll see you in a couple of days."

Jeff hurried out the door to the cheers of the crowd in the dining room. The smile spreading across his lips almost made his face hurt, but he was happy. For the first time in a long time, he was happy.

After jumping in his truck and turning the key for the third time, he knew he had a problem. It wouldn't start. His old reliable Chevy wouldn't start. *Fuck!* He banged his hand on the steering wheel before he pushed open the door and then slammed it shut again.

He raced for the lodge to borrow his parents' truck. *Damn it. I'm not letting her get away.*

When he hit the door, he almost ran into his mother coming out. "Problem?"

"I can't get my truck to start."

She pulled the keys to theirs from her pocket. "Go!"

"Thanks, Mom." He kissed her on the cheek before rushing around the edge of the building to where their truck sat.

Within seconds he tore down the gravel driveway silently asking for forgiveness at tearing up the rocks on his way out. He hit the gate opener on the visor above his head, early enough to watch the wrought iron metal swing just wide enough for the truck to get through.

The ride to Houston would take three plus hours. He had a lot of time on his hands to think about what he would say to her besides I love you. What did you say to a woman who thought you didn't trust her? I'm sorry would be a good starter, he figured. Then I love you. He shook his head. He needed to beg for her forgiveness. Tell her he trusted her and loved her with all his heart.

"Damn, this is getting sappier by the minute."

Flowers. Good idea.

He'd stop somewhere along the way to get a dozen roses. *Hell.* He didn't even know what flowers she liked, what her favorite color was or anything. What about her family? Did she have siblings? Were her parents still alive?

Doubts began to surface. How could he love someone he knew so little about? Yeah, they were good in bed together and they could learn more about each other over time, but what really did they have to build a relationship on?

"She loves Ben. There's a start. It's a hell of a lot more than Misha had and she gave birth to him." He sighed. "I'll learn about her. We can spend the next two days talkin'."

Yeah right.

"Okay, makin' love and then talkin'."

Before he knew it he was on the interstate headed for Houston singing along with the radio. His fingers tapped along with the beat while he wondered if she might have the radio on in her car. What if he called the station and dedicated a song to her? Would she hear it? Would she care?

He grabbed his cell phone from the clip on his belt and dialed. Luck seemed to be on his side when the DJ picked up.

"KJ Country what can I do for you?"

"Listen, man. I need a huge favor. I'm chasin' a girl down to tell her I love her and I want to see if you'll play a song in case she's listenin'."

"Sure, man. How about I record you and we'll get it over the airwaves in the next fifteen minutes."

"You are fantastic." He breathed in through his nose and out through his mouth. "Okay. I'm ready."

"I'll do a little intro and then I'll have you come on. What's your name, dude?"

"Jeff Young."

"All righty, Jeff. Ready?"

"Yeah."

"Well folks, we have a brokenhearted cowboy on the line wanting to dedicate a song to one special lady friend. Are ya there, Jeff?"

"Yes, sir."

"Go ahead, man."

"I want to send Cowboys and Angels out to Terri Kennedy. We had a bit of a misunderstanding and she's headed back home to Houston right now. Terri, baby, I love you and I don't care if I have to chase you across the map. I'm gonna find you and tell you in person how much I love you."

"Cool man. I hope you catch her."

"Thanks, bro. You're the best."

They clicked off the recording and the DJ came back on the line. "Thanks, Jeff. I hope you catch your lady friend."

"Oh, I will sooner or later, but thanks for running the song for me. She's my angel and I can't wait to hold her again."

"Good luck."

"Thanks."

Jeff clicked off the phone and waited during the longest fifteen minutes of his life for the song to come on. *Then what?*

When the DJ came on, he heard his voice as he held his breath.

Chapter Thirteen

Tears had long ago dried on her face during the drive toward home. She wouldn't cry anymore for him. *Damn him!* Falling in love with him was the stupidest thing she could have done, but alas, it happened and she would have to deal with it for the rest of her life. Maybe someday she would find someone to take his place. Somehow she wasn't so sure.

She inhaled a sharp, weary sigh and reached over to turn on the radio. Maybe a little music would help. "I hope they don't play a bunch of sappy love songs. I sure don't need those right now."

A few songs later she found herself tapping her fingers on the steering wheel in rhythm to Save a Horse, Ride a Cowboy. It wasn't a sappy song, but it still reminded her of Jeff.

Will everything remind me of him?

"Probably for a hell of a long time to come."

"Hey, folks. I have a special request from a lonely cowboy. He's got a plea for a special lady. Take a listen and I hope she hears this. We recorded this a few minutes ago."

Terri half listened as the DJ's recording came on.

"Well, folks, we have a brokenhearted cowboy on the line wanting to dedicate a song to one special lady friend. Are ya there, Jeff?"

"Yes, sir."

"Go ahead, man."

"I want to send Cowboys and Angels out to Terri Kennedy. We had a bit of a misunderstanding and she's headed back home to Houston right now. Terri, baby, I love you and I don't care if I have to chase you across the map. I'm gonna find you and tell you in person how much I love you."

"Cool man. I hope you catch her."

"Thanks, bro. You're the best."

Her heart pounded in her ears. Did she just hear what she thought she heard? Jeff on the radio saying he loved her?

She fumbled with her purse, trying to grab her cell phone without crashing her car. When she checked her phonebook, she cussed under her breath. She didn't have his number!

The DJ came back on. "Terri if you're listenin', darlin', give me a call here at the station. I want to find out what happens between you and Jeff. Of course, you can wait until you actually hook up with him somewhere along the highway." The guy rattled off the number as he laughed and then moved onto something else.

Her hands shook. She wasn't sure what to do as she continued to drive along at seventy miles an hour toward home. She couldn't call him. She could call the ranch and ask for his number. *Hmm.* What should she do? Call the station and hope he was still listening on his end of the radio dial? Should she wait until she got home? No, she couldn't do that. It would drive her nuts to wait that long.

She quickly dialed the radio station.

"KJ Country."

"I'm Terri Kennedy."

"Well hello, Terri Kennedy."

"Is this the DJ who talked to Jeff?"

"Yes, ma'am."

"I can't call him. I don't have his number."

"Where are you, darlin'?"

"On the interstate about an hour out of San Antonio. Can you do me a favor?"

"Sure, honey."

She glanced at the roadside sign as a plan formed in her head. "Get on the radio and tell Jeff to meet me in the parking lot of the Quickie Mart off the highway." She rattled off the exit number to the DJ, thanked him and hung up, then waited for him to come on the radio.

The exit came into view and she pulled her car off the highway to wait. *God, this wait is gonna kill me for sure.* If he just left San Antonio, it would be probably forty-five minutes before he would get off the exit and they would know whether what he said came from the heart or not.

The DJ came on the radio again and put her message out there for all of San Antonio to hear. She hoped Jeff heard it. *What if he didn't? What if he thought when I didn't call that I don't love him too or I don't care if he loves me? What about the trust thing? He probably still thinks I'm working for the developers and out to ruin him and his family. The financial information seemed to be a stickler for him, but all I wanted was information to make sure they were secure enough financially to fight the developers in court if need be.*

Terri sat in her car watching the off ramp for his beat up Chevy truck. The minutes ticked off slower than molasses in June. Every few minutes, she cursed the slow time.

Several cars, trucks, and big rigs got off the exit, but no Jeff.

"What the hell? Shouldn't he be here by now?"

A black dully pickup was the next one off the exit, coming at her like a bat out of hell. It drove straight for her car, almost looking like the driver didn't plan to stop until he ran over the hood of her car.

The driver stopped at her front bumper, but didn't exit the truck.

Terri held her breath. *Jeff doesn't drive a black truck.*

Her heart pounded in her ears as she waited.

The door opened and a guy in a black Stetson stepped out.

Her mouth went dry.

Jeff.

She opened her door and rushed around the doorframe straight into his arms.

The minute their lips met in a heart-melting kiss, a huge roar of applause erupted around them.

They broke apart long enough to see a hundred people surrounding them clapping and cheering.

Heat crawled up her neck and splashed across her cheeks in embarrassment. Apparently, all these people heard them on the radio as they hollered congratulations.

"Come back to the ranch with me."

"But…"

"But what? I'm guessin' you heard me on the radio."

"I did, but I want to hear it from you."

"I love you, Terri. You own my heart." He cupped her face. "We can work out the rest later."

"The rest?"

"Do you love me?" he asked, fear clear in his gray eyes.

She threw her arms around his neck and held on tight. "Yes. God, yes. I love you with all my heart."

"Good. Everything will work itself out then."

"I'm not sure I know what you mean."

He kissed her eyes, both cheeks and then pressed a quick one to her lips. "A few facts I realized I don't know about you is all, darlin'. I know enough to know I love you and want you in my life."

"And Ben?"

"He loves you. He already asked me when I was gonna ask you to be his new momma."

"I would love to be his new momma."

"We'll plan the rest later. Right now we need to find somewhere so I can love you like I want to."

"Why don't we wait until we get to my place? I have a great bed."

"You'll move home with me?"

Trepidation rushed through her. What if he still didn't trust her? "What about the trust thing?"

"Mom told me what you did for me…for the family. I still don't understand why you needed the financial information, but finding the rare bird was priceless. I would have loved to seen the developer's face when you told him his land was worthless to build on."

"I wanted to make sure your family was financially secure enough to fight them in court if need be. It could still go to court, Jeff, but the wildlife resource committee is on your side. The last thing they want is to have to try to relocate a rare bird's nesting ground for some home developers. The judge they got to sign the order declaring it a wildlife refuge is fully onboard with the whole thing. He knows the drill."

"All thanks to you."

"There are a few more things we need to talk about with your family's property, Jeff. I found a few other things that might be of interest."

He pressed his fingers to her lips. "Later, darlin'. Right now I want nothin' more than to sink into your sweet heat and never come out, but we certainly can't do that here in the parking lot of the Quickie Mart."

A giggle left her lips. "You're right, but how am I supposed to drive home knowing you're behind me all hard and waiting?" She shifted her hips, brushing her pelvis against his erection. "All for me?"

He hissed as a low growl left his lips. "You'll pay for torturing me."

"Oh, I certainly hope so."

* * * *

Terri groaned as she rolled over and opened her eyes. Sunlight poured through the blinds on her window. Jeff lay on his stomach next to her with his head buried in the pillow, snoring softly. They didn't go to sleep for a long time after they reached her apartment. Loving a cowboy definitely had its perks.

The tattoo on his shoulder blade caught her attention. She'd seen it before, but the night he'd slept in her cabin, he'd been in such a rush to get out before anyone saw him, she hadn't had a chance to examine it closely.

The dragon started on his shoulder blade and ended with its tail wrapped around his upper arm like a tribal tattoo. It suited him to a T. Ben's name graced the arch of the dragon's back. A tribute to the love this man had for his son. She slowly traced the nose of the dragon with her finger, loving the feel of his skin under her touch.

"You're gonna make me hard again, you know," he said, without opening his eyes.

The little quirk of his lips made her heart race. "I hope so." She leaned over to kiss the tattoo. "I love how you have Ben's name on your back."

"He's my life." He rolled over and pulled her into his arms so her head rested on his chest. "Now, you're my life too."

"I know, Jeff."

He kissed the top of her head as he trailed a fingertip down her arm. "You know. I don't know much about you at all. Family? Where do your parents live?"

"South of Houston. Santa Fe actually."

"Siblings?"

"One brother."

"Will it be strange for you to be a part of such a big family?"

She laughed, propping herself up on her elbow to look into his eyes. "Are you kidding me? I've always wanted to have more brothers or sisters, but my mom got cervical cancer and had to have a complete hysterectomy."

"I hope she's okay now."

"She is. She's been cancer free for ten years. I count every day with her as a blessing."

"I bet."

She laid her head back on his chest.

"Where were you born?"

"Houston. I've lived there all my life. Santa Fe is just south of Houston."

"What's your favorite color?"

"Blue. What about you?"

"Green."

"You aren't saying that because my eyes are green, are you?"

"They are? I hadn't noticed."

She punched him in the side before he rolled her over onto her back and straddled her hips. She didn't even have time to blink. The scruff on his cheeks deliciously abraded her skin as he kissed her neck, across her shoulder and then scooted down to nuzzle her breast.

"I want your ass, Terri."

His lips on her nipple made her shiver. Goose bumps flittered across her body in a wave, from the top of her head to the tips of her toes. "Like smacking it or what?"

"No, I wanna fuck it." His words sounded muffled against the skin of her breast.

Her nipple hardened under the rough slide of his tongue. "Did you say you want to fuck it?"

He lifted his head as his eyes seemed to dance with the flame of need. "Yeah. Will you let me?"

"If you promise to make sure things are well lubed. I've never had a man there before."

"Sure, baby. I would never do anything to hurt you. I'll make sure you're so excited, you'll beg me."

She giggled. "Beg, huh?" Nerves wracked her body, but she trusted Jeff. She loved him so if he wanted to do her ass, she'd work with it.

"Oh yeah."

His hand slipped down her abdomen to play in the curls at the juncture of her thighs. "Open for me."

She spread her legs as she sighed her pleasure when his fingers pushed inside her pussy. *God, I love this man more than life itself.* "Please."

"Please what?"

"More."

He quickly spun around into a sixty-nine position before he slid his lips down her body, stopping momentarily to flick his tongue around her belly button before continuing down to bury his face between her thighs. She cupped his balls, rolling the hard little nuggets between her fingers. He moaned deep in his throat. The sound reverberated against her skin.

The rough pad of his tongue felt like heaven on her swollen, heated tissues. At the rate he was eating her out, she wouldn't last long before she came undone in a high scream loud enough to wake the neighbors. "God, Jeff."

He shoved two fingers deep inside her and pumped the digits until she felt her pussy clamp down on them. Her wail of ecstasy sounded primal with need. Never mind she'd already had this man twice the night before.

One finger spread the juices from her pussy to her ass. She shivered as he slowly pushed one finger past the ring of muscles. The intrusion burned slightly, but wasn't completely unpleasant. His tongue made a return trip to her clit, flicking the distended button back and forth until she felt on fire again.

"Easy, baby."

"Feels weird."

"Weird good or weird bad?"

"Good."

He pushed two fingers inside her ass as she hissed at the burn. "You okay?"

"Yeah. Burns a little."

The slow crawl of his fingers soothed the ache, but also brought it higher at the same time. A different need took its place.

"Do you happen to have some lube around?"

"Yeah, in my nightstand. I needed it sometimes before. I kind of get dry."

"You ain't dry with me, sweetheart." He spread more of her juices around her clit. "You're soaking wet."

"Because you wind me up so much, I can't wait to get you inside me."

He removed his fingers and turned so he was positioned between her legs. She tensed up. "Easy, darlin'. We won't do anything without lube." He grabbed the tube from her drawer and placed it on the bed beside them. "I'm gonna fuck your pussy a little before we move on. I love to feel you squeeze me."

"Oh yeah." Her words came out in a soft purr as he pushed his length inside her. No condom. "Uh, Jeff?"

"Yeah, babe?"

"Did you forget a condom?"

"Do we need one?"

"I'm not on birth control. I haven't been active with anyone in a long time so I didn't need it. What if we get pregnant?"

"Do you want to?"

She smoothed his hair back from his forehead. "I've love to have a baby with you, but we haven't really talked about the future of this relationship yet."

"I want you with me."

"I know you do. I love you and I really believe you love me too, but what happens next?"

He shifted his hips. "Can we talk about this after we're done?"

"No." She moved so his cock wasn't penetrating her anymore. "We need to talk about this now."

"Fuck."

"Do you love me?"

"Yes."

"Say it."

"I love you, Terri. I told you that before."

"So what are your plans for our future?"

"I don't know. I thought you'd move back to the ranch with me. We can be a family."

"Do you ever plan to marry me?"

"Marriage? Wait a minute."

"That's what I thought." She pushed against his chest until she could slide out from under him. "I think you need to leave."

"Leave? I'm not leaving."

"Yes, you are. Go back to the ranch or whatever. I don't care."

"I thought you said you loved me?"

"I do, Jeff. I love you with all my heart, but I'm not shacking up with you until hell freezes over because you're scared to get married again or live in a long term relationship with the intention of marriage at some point."

He jumped to his feet, grabbed his pants and then shoved his legs into them. "So this is all to get a marriage proposal out of me?"

"Fuck off!"

His chest rose and fell with his rapid breaths. A sheen of sweat coated his upper lip. The man was in full panic attack mode at just the thought of getting married. "I ain't leavin' until we talk about this."

"There's nothing to talk about."

"Come on, Terri. I love you. Isn't that enough?"

"No, it's not, Jeff. I'm sorry, but it's not. I want to get married someday. Have a family. Raise my kids with the man who helped me produce them. I'm not going anywhere. You don't trust me."

"Yes, I do."

"No, not really. You say you love me, but the trust isn't there."

"What can I do to change your mind about this?"

"Ask me to marry you."

"I can't." He threw up his hands and let them fall. Dejection clouded his eyes.

"I know," she whispered in a tearful voice. *Am I doing the right thing? What if he walks away and never comes back? What if I never see him again?* A twenty pound lump clogged her throat. She slipped on her bathrobe, uncomfortable now with her nakedness in front of him.

He raked his fingers through his hair. "This isn't over."

She glanced at the ceiling as she pressed her lips together to keep from telling him it didn't matter, when in truth it mattered a great deal.

Chapter Fourteen

Jeff pulled his parent's truck into the driveway of the ranch, hit the gate button on the visor and sighed. What the hell went wrong? He loved Terri, but here he was returning to the ranch without her. This whole thing seemed totally fucked up.

"Daddy!" Ben raced from the door of the main house toward the truck as Jeff put it into park.

Nina followed closely on his heels, but her lips turned down in a frown when she saw the passenger side of the truck was empty. "Is Terri following you in her car?" she asked as he stepped out and shut the door.

"No, Mom."

"What happened?"

"I can't talk about it right now."

"Yes, you can and you will." She hollered toward the barn for his father who poked his head out of the double doors. "Can you take Ben please? I need to have a chat with our son."

"Uh-oh. You in trouble, Daddy?"

"I guess so, buddy. Go on with Granddad."

Ben raced across the yard as fast as his little legs would carry him.

"Come with me."

Apparently he was in for the talking to of his life with his mom and he couldn't bring up the feelings to care. He'd left his heart in Houston, but he wasn't sure what the hell to do about it. Marry Terri? His stomach rolled at the thought. Not that he didn't want to be with her. He did. More than anything, but marriage? Tied down to her for the rest of his life? What if she turned out to be like Misha? What if she cheated on him?

"Now," his mother said, pointing to the chair in her office for him to sit. "What is this all about?"

"Terri told me to leave."

"Well you spent the night with her last night, right?"

"Yeah." He raked his fingers through his hair, knocking off his hat in the process. "I don't get her, Ma."

"You love her, right?"

"Yeah and she said she loves me."

"Then what is the problem here?"

"She wants a marriage proposal."

"And?" His mother had a look of *are you stupid or what* on her face.

"I can't do it, Ma. I won't. What if somethin' happens again?"

"So what, Jeffery," she clasped his hands between hers, "honey, you're in love with her. She's in love with you. Marriage is the next logical step. You can't live your life worrying about if it's going to fall apart, sweetheart. You'll be miserable for the rest of your life if you do. Do you seriously want to let the hell Misha put you through ruin your future?"

"No."

"You have to move on. Terri is your future. The future for you and Ben." She ran one hand down his cheek and came away with wet fingers. "You'll be miserable without her. Don't you trust her?"

"I'm not sure."

"Why are you crying?"

"Because I miss her. I need her with me."

"You'll have to get over this fear you have then. I don't think she's going to settle for anything besides a marriage proposal from you." She patted his hand. "Take a few days to think about it, son. I think you'll come to the same conclusion I have."

She walked out leaving him with his thoughts. Everything seemed jumbled and out of focus. His life was up in the air all of the sudden. Yes, he still had his job on the ranch. The future of the ranch appeared secure thanks to Terri. His heart would never be the same without her in his life.

He sighed and let his head fall back against the wall behind him. What to do? What did he want from Terri? A friends with benefits situation? No. That didn't seem right either. He loved her. He knew he did, but could he get past his fear of marriage and a committed relationship to secure the future with her she wanted?

"Daddy?" Ben put his hand on his leg. "Did you ask Ms. Terri to be my new momma?"

"No, Ben, I didn't."

"Why not? I want her to come live with us."

"I want her to live with us too, buddy."

"Then why isn't she here?"

"It's complicated."

"You love her?"

"Yeah."

"Then it's not comli...whatever you said. You just bring her back here."

Jeff laughed. Oh to have the simplicity of life of a three-year-old. *Just bring her back here.* Could he? Would it be as easy as that?

A plan began to form in his head. He needed some help from one of his brothers, but he needed to think about what his future held without her before he planned a future with her in it. The bleakness without her choked the life from his heart.

"Let's go home, buddy."

"Okay." Ben rushed out toward the front room but stopped short.

"What's wrong?"

"The ghost man is sitting in the chair over there, Daddy."

Sure enough, Jeff could see the figure of an older gentleman in cowboy clothes sitting on the leather couch near the fireplace. He tipped his hat and faded away. Shivers raced down his back. He'd never get used to seeing the ghosts around the house no matter how many times he ran into them.

Jeff took Ben's hand as they walked through the dining room headed back outside. He had some thinking to do and some plans to make. Within minutes they were pulling up to the front of his small cabin. He knew no one waited for him to come home. The house needed a woman's touch. Even when he'd been married to Misha, she'd never done anything to make it a home. The small things counted like flowers in window boxes, fluffy white curtains blowing in the breeze at the kitchen window, and a pretty comforter on the bed, even pillow shams would make it more homey. What would Terri do to the place should he get her to come home with him? Would she want to make it hers like he hoped or would she turn into a shrew like Misha who didn't want his home, his child or his family?

Terri wasn't like that.

He opened the door to help Ben out of his car seat and get him down. His son ran for the front door, pushing it open in a rush. Since they didn't have anyone to come home to, the house looked forlorn.

"Bath time, Ben," Jeff called to his retreating son.

"No."

"Yes."

"No."

Jeff sighed. Times like this, he wanted someone in his life more than anything, someone to take over mommy duties so he didn't have to fight with the kid every night.

Ben ran past him, but Jeff grabbed him up in a bear hug and headed for the bathroom with the wiggling, giggling child in his arms. He got Ben into the bathroom and stripped off his clothes before he turned on the water. The bathroom looked like a typical kid's bathroom with thousands of toys in the tub. The naked kid tried to dash out the door, but Jeff got it shut with his boot before Ben escaped in a naked streak down the hall.

As he plopped the kid in the water, a knock sounded on the door. *Who the hell could that be?*

"I'll be right there!" He looked at Ben. What the hell to do? He only had two hands and a wet, wiggling child took precedence over whoever was at the door. No way would he leave Ben alone in the bathtub.

He shut the water off, wrapped Ben in a towel and propped him on his hip. This is just what he needed.

Opening the door with a sharp snap, he asked, "Yeah?"

The last person he thought he'd see standing on his doorstep spun around on her heels.

"Terri?"

"Hi." She pressed her lips together. "Can I come in?"

"Uh, sure." He stepped back.

"Hi, Ms. Terri!"

"Hiya, Ben. Bath time?"

"No."

"Yes," Jeff said with a laugh. "I was just getting him into the tub."

"I can wait until you're done." She laid her purse on the end table next to the couch.

His gaze slide down her frame, taking in the tank top curving around her breasts as it clung to every inch of her delicious body.

"Go take care of your son. I'll be right here."

Jeff disappeared down the hall with the squirming Ben in his arms. Tonight would be the fastest bath in history of bathing a child, he vowed. He put Ben in the tub, quickly washed his hair and body before he took the handheld showerhead down off the wall and rinsed him off. "Okay, Ben, out we go."

"I wanna play."

"Nope. Not tonight, buddy. Bedtime for you."

"But I wanna play."

Jeff sighed. The kid was going to drive him nuts before he reached his fifth birthday. He had other things to do tonight. Terri was here and he'd be damned if he let her go again.

* * * *

Terri smiled at the splashing sounds coming from the bathroom as she waited for Jeff to finish bathing Ben. She hadn't really thought this trip through when she'd gotten into her car to drive back out to the ranch to confront Jeff. She'd come to some conclusions after he'd given up and walked out of her life earlier in the day. It hadn't taken her more than an hour of soul searching to realize giving him the ultimatum of a marriage proposal or nothing wasn't right on her part. The gun-shy guy she loved didn't do well with choices like that.

What the hell am I gonna do if he doesn't want me here? "Surely if he didn't, he wouldn't have let me in the door."

She glanced around the living room realizing she hadn't had time to check out the home she hoped to share with the amazing man in the other room. The dark décor and lack of feminine touches didn't surprise her. His ex-wife didn't come across as a very family oriented woman from what she knew of her, although granted that wasn't much. Terri started picturing the little things she'd do to the house to make it more of a home. Some flowers outside. Curtains on the windows. A nice comforter on the bed. Toy Story curtains on Ben's window. It was obvious Jeff didn't bother with anything except the bare necessities.

Realizing the sounds coming from the bathroom had quieted, her stomach knotted in anticipation. She stood and moved toward the fireplace. She put one elbow up on the mantle, and took it down. Then twisted her fingers into a ball of knotted flesh. *Damn, I'm nervous.* Her stomach rolled, making her nauseous. It wouldn't bode well if she puked up her dinner before she even had a chance to talk to him.

She exhaled on a sigh to try to calm her stomach. It didn't work very well. Her heart thumped against her ribs like a terrified bird in a cage.

The sound of his boot steps coming down the hall didn't help her nervousness, but the time had come to answer some questions.

He stopped in the doorway and took in her entire body as a small smile played on those oh-so-kissable lips. *God, is it bad I want to curl myself around him and stay there forever?*

A nervous wipe of his hands down his thighs gave away his true feelings about her being there too as he walked into the living room. "Why don't you have a seat?"

"I would, but I'm nervous."

"Why?" he asked, taking a seat on the couch.

"Because I didn't know whether you'd hear me out. I rehearsed this whole long speech on the way here, but seeing you made every bit of it slip straight out of my head."

"Is that a good thing?"

She smiled and shrugged, taking a seat on the other side of the couch. "Maybe."

The silence stretched between them for several minutes while she tried to think of what to say since her speech didn't mean anything now. "I'm sorry. I guess I should start with that."

"Sorry for what?"

"Pressuring you. That wasn't fair to you. I know how hard it is for you to trust and we really haven't known each other very long." She twisted the ring on her right hand. It was one her mother gave her on her sixteenth birthday and she never took it off.

"No, we haven't." He seemed relaxed now as he stretched his arm across the back of the sofa.

"Are you sure you love me?" she asked, hoping he hadn't changed his mind.

"Yeah, but it's gonna take some time for me to get to the marriage part. I ain't sayin' I'll never get there, Terri."

"I guess it's all I'll get for now, huh?"

"No. I want you to be part of my life. I want you to move in here with me and Ben."

"Are you sure? I mean, isn't it kind of a big move?"

"Not as big as marriage."

"True."

"We'll keep everythin' separate. You can come and go like you want. I won't expect you to take over the house like you're my wife or anythin' if you don't want to."

"What if I want to?"

"Then you can. I want us to be more than just roommates with benefits." He smiled. "I like the benefits parts though."

"Can I do some decorating here? Nothing major. Curtains, flowers…things like that."

"Sure you can, darlin'."

Her heart tripped over itself when she heard his endearment. He hadn't given up on her completely, but she'd earn his trust and his long term love. If he never asked her to marry him, it was really okay. She'd have him in her life and that was the most important part of the whole thing.

"Come 'ere."

She launched herself into his arms, kissing all over his face in a rush to reach his lips. The softness of his mouth against hers brought tears to her eyes. "I love you."

"I love you too, Terri. Don't ever forget that no matter what, okay? I want you in my life."

"I want to be there too."

"Good. When can you move your stuff in?"

"I'll have to pack up my apartment, but I brought enough with me to stay for a while."

"Awful confident weren't you?" he asked, pushing his fingers into her hair.

"Hell no. I planned on staying in one of the cabins at the ranch until you said you loved me again."

He kissed her quickly, a little smooch that left her wanting a lot more. "I never stopped, baby. I just can't commit to marriage right now."

She ran her tongue across his jaw, enjoying the stubble of the unshaven line. "I know and I'm sorry I pushed you. It wasn't fair to you."

"Will you stay with me tonight?"

"If you want me to."

"Yeah, I do. The thought of not havin' you in my bed tonight had me goin' crazy." His gray eyes reflected the love he felt for her.

After all, a ring didn't mean anything. The feelings between two people resided in their hearts. "You can have me every night in your bed with no strings. I promise not to pressure you anymore about a ring."

"I hope you know how much I love you."

"You mean everything to me, Jeff. I've never felt this way about anyone before and I don't plan on feeling this way about anyone ever again. You're it for me."

He pushed her back, forcing her to stand. "Come on. I've got a woman to love on for the next hundred years."

"Only a hundred?" she asked with a giggle as he swept her up into his arms and headed for his bedroom.

"We'll start there."

"I can do a hundred or a thousand. As long as I'm with you, it doesn't matter how many years go by. We'll be together."

"In this house, in this bed. Together. Just the two of us."

"Or three depending on how many times Ben ends up in bed with us."

"Oh, he might too. He does tend to crawl into bed with me when he has a nightmare or something. Since he has a new momma, he might tend to be there more than we want him to be."

"I'm sure he'll get over it soon enough," she said as he gently laid her down on the comforter.

He stripped off his shirt, revealing the smattering of chest hair to her gaze. She loved running her fingers through the springy curls. The belt buckle and jeans came next, leaving her to take in his hard cock as he pushed everything to the floor. She loved having all that hard flesh inside her. Would he want her ass this time since they'd been interrupted before? She kind of hoped so. She wanted to feel everything with him.

"Take off your clothes."

She sat up on the bed on her knees and pulled the tank top over her head. The softness in his eyes as he took in her body told her more than anything how much he loved her. She laid back down to remove her shorts in one swoop. Luckily, she left her sandals in the living room when she'd taken a seat on the couch.

"God, you're beautiful."

"You aren't so bad yourself, cowboy."

His cock bobbed against his stomach, begging for her touch or her mouth in a little dance she wasn't sure he didn't orchestrate just to torment her. She wanted both. With her hand wrapped around his length, she took him between her lips and sucked the head.

A soft moan broke from his mouth. "I love when you suck me."

She took him deeper, swallowing as much of his length as she could. He wasn't a small man by any means.

His hips shifted, pushing more of him into her mouth. He wrapped his hands in her hair, pulling slightly. The sting of his tug made her weak and wet. She didn't realize how much rough sex turned her on, until Jeff came along.

He reached over to land a heavy smack on her ass cheek. The pain of his heavy hand had juices dripping down the inside of her leg.

"Enough." He pulled her back by her hair until she released his cock. "I don't want to come in your mouth. I want so much more from you."

"Like what, cowboy?"

"Your pussy, your ass. Can we make it a triple penetration night?"

"Maybe. Goin' for the trifecta huh?"

"You bet. Spread them legs for me, babe." His cock pushed against her opening. "You okay with no condom?"

"Yes. I trust you, but I'll see about birth control in the next few weeks."

"Do you want a baby with me?"

"Of course, I do. I love you, but I think we should wait a bit."

"Then let's use the condom until you're on something to keep it from happenin' until we're ready."

He grabbed one from the nightstand drawer and rolled it on. "It's not foolproof, but it's better than nothin'."

"If it happens, it happens, Jeff. It's God's will if we make a baby even using a condom."

The slow penetration of his cock drove her wild. She loved having him inside her. Her swollen tissues stretched to accommodate his size as her pussy dampened even more.

"I love bein' inside you."

"I like it too. Fuck me, Jeff. Give it to me hard. I need this more than you know."

He shoved inside her in one thrust, tearing a groan from deep in her chest. The rapid push of his thrusts had her on edge in seconds. "Yes," she whispered in a rapid mantra to the rhythm of his pace. Heat crawled up her legs in a rush to reach her pelvis. The burst of sensation ripped a moan from her lips as she came in a heated gush.

"Now, I want your ass," he said, as she slowly came down from her orgasm.

"Lube."

"Got it." He grabbed a tube from the nightstand drawer and set it on the bed next to her.

"Tell me what to do."

"Roll over onto your stomach."

When he had her positioned how he wanted, she heard the squirt of lubrication and felt the liquid on her ass. "Damn, that's cold."

"Sorry, I should have warmed it up a little."

"It's okay." He spread the wet slickness around her anus before he shoved a finger past the ring of muscles. The burn felt odd, but not too bad this time.

"Ready for two?"

"Okay." Her ass contracted around his fingers when he stick two inside and scissored them to stretch her hole.

"Are you all right?"

"Yeah." She pushed back against the invasion, wanting more. "I need more."

More lube ran down the crack of her ass as he spread it inside. "Ready for me?"

"I guess. Just go slowly."

"Sure, babe. You can drive this train."

The feel of having his cock bumped at her ass and then slowly push inside felt like hell. *The burn!* "Wait."

He stopped pushing.

She breathed through the pain. "Okay."

He moved a little more. "Okay?"

"Yeah. I want to push back against you."

"Good. That's what you're supposed to feel. Do what you want. I'm almost all the way inside."

"Really? Wow."

She pushed back taking the rest of him inside until she felt the hair at his groin touch her butt. "Oh my God!"

"Pretty intense, huh?"

"Oh, hell yeah." She wiggled her butt.

"You're gonna kill me woman. I can't hold still much longer."

"I don't want you too. Fuck me, Jeff."

He slowly drew his cock out, and then just as slowly pushed back in. The sensation was something she couldn't even describe. The burn had disappeared with the deliberate slide of his cock in and out of her ass.

"Faster."

"You sure?"

"Yeah, please."

He increased the pace of his thrust, pulling a tortured moan from her mouth. The gritty sound torn from her lips felt foreign, but good. It felt incredible to share this with him. Something she'd never given to another man in her entire life, only to give it to the man she loved with her whole heart.

One of his hands snaked around her hip to run a finger over her clit. Her whole body vibrated with need. She had to come soon or the top of her head would explode into a splattering mess all over his bed.

"Come for me, darlin'."

Stars exploded in her head as her body detonated into a thousand tiny particles of sensation. Every nerve ending in her body prickled like tiny electrical charges on her skin.

Jeff moaned softly as his hips pistoned at an uncoordinated rhythm meant to bring him to satisfaction. She wanted it, needed to feel him come hard and enjoy the fulfilling intimacy they'd just shared.

"Oh God," he whispered as his body shivered against her backside and then collapsed along her back, driving them both to the bed in a heap.

"Good for you?" she asked with a laugh.

"Hell yeah."

"I thought so."

"Did you like it? I mean if you didn't we don't have to do it again, but I thought…"

"I loved it, Jeff. You made it special. It wasn't something I'd been able to trust anyone with before now, but you are the man I love. I want to experience everything with you."

"I love you, Terri."

"Good. Now, I think you need to clean up and I know I do. All this cum and goo between my legs is sticky."

"Shower?"

"Hmm. That would be great especially if you'll join me."

"I wouldn't miss it."

He pulled his cock from her ass and stood, then helped her stand too. "First one in gets to adjust the temperature," he said, racing for the bathroom.

"Women first, mister!"

The laughter ringing through the house brought goose bumps to her body. She'd found the man she could love for the rest of her life. She sent up a silent thank you to God for helping her see the error of pushing him too far too fast. He would come around in time, but for now, loving him and Ben, building a family with them would take up all the time she had.

Epilogue

Christmas was a time for family. The family she'd built with Jeff and Ben meant everything to her. She'd moved her business to Bandera and had to finally take time off from work to spend the season with them.

The four-year-old child of her heart sat by the Christmas tree bouncing on his butt waiting for his father to say he could open the mountain of presents.

"Now, Daddy?"

"Nope. Wait just a minute." Jeff crawled on the floor toward the tree and sat down next to the boxes. "Okay now I'll give you one at a time to open."

She smiled. The amount of presents under there probably set her back a pretty penny, but she didn't care. This was their first Christmas as a family.

"This is from, Grandma and Granddad."

The brightly wrapped box became a shred of paper within seconds and he squealed in delight at his present. "More?"

"Slow down, buddy, or you'll have them all opened so fast, it'll be over."

Ben frowned. The next present was opened a little piece of paper at a time. Another squeal at the train set she'd bought with Jeff brought a smile to her lips. He still loved Toy Story, but Thomas the Train was quickly becoming his new favorite thing. Kids.

She had a special surprise for Jeff, but it would have to wait until Ben went to bed.

Within thirty minutes, all the presents under the tree were opened. Ben jumped up and hugged Terri, bringing tears to her eyes. "Thank you, Momma. Thank you, Daddy."

"You're welcome, honey," she said, hugging him right back. Her love for this little boy grew every day.

"Time for bed."

"No."

"Yes," Jeff said. "Santa won't come if you don't go to bed."

Ben looked at her with wide eyes. "Off to bed with you, Ben."

"All right."

Jeff laughed and she smiled. They went through this ritual almost every night. Jeff would tell him to do something, but as soon as Terri told him to do it, he'd automatically say yes and off he'd go.

"I'll be right back." Jeff grabbed Ben, tossed him over his shoulder to the gleeful squeals of the boy and off to bed they went.

Nervousness gripped her stomach. How would he feel when she gave him his present?

Within moments, he returned to take the seat next to her on the couch and wrap her in his arms. He winced a little, drawing her concern. "Are you okay?"

"Yeah, why?"

"You're acting like you're in pain."

"Well, it's a surprise."

"Really? What kind of surprise?"

"First I need to give you your gift." He grabbed a small box from the end table, she hadn't noticed before. "Open it."

Anticipation coiled her nerves. It looked like a jewelry box of some sort. *Dare I hope?*

The blue velvet box shook in her hands as she slowly slid open the top. A gorgeous diamond necklace winked back at her with two hearts entwined.

"Oh my."

"Do you like it? I thought it signified what we have at least for now. I love you so much, I wish I could express it more."

"Baby, you do every day in how you treat me and love me. It's beautiful. It's perfect. Will you put it on?"

She spun around to let him clasp the necklace behind her neck. When she turned back, she saw tears in his eyes.

"There's one more thing. I hope it means as much to you as it does to me." He pulled his T-shirt over his head and turned around. There on his tattoo was her name next to Ben's, the skin still raw and red from application.

"Oh Jeff." To have him ink her name on his body meant the world to her. It wasn't an engagement ring, but it almost meant more. He'd accepted her as a permanent part of his life just as he accepted the permanent ink on his body. "Thank you."

He spun around and kissed her. Her world tipped on its axis as he stuck his tongue into her mouth and dueled with hers. A moan escaped her lips, but she couldn't get caught up in his kiss just yet.

She pushed him away and smiled at the exasperated look on his face. "You already opened your gift from me."

"And I love the new belt buckle with our names engraved on it. It's great."

"Thanks, but there is one more thing and I hope you're okay with it."

"I'll love anything you have to give me, baby. I hope you know that."

"What about a baby?" she asked as she bit her lip.

"A baby?"

"Yeah. I know we didn't plan this, but I'm pregnant."

"Seriously? Wow."

A slow smile spread across his lips, bringing down her anxiety to a tolerable level. "You're okay with this?"

"I would love to have a baby with you, Terri. I'll love any child we have between us whether it be another ornery little boy like Ben or a beautiful little girl who looks just like her mother." He pulled her onto his lap. "When did you find out?"

"A couple of days ago."

"When will he or she be born?"

"I don't have an actual due date yet since I haven't been to the doctor, but sometime late summer."

He kissed her in a slow, loving kiss of two hearts beating as one.

The End

About the Author

Sandy Sullivan is a romance author, who, when not writing, spends her time with her husband Shaun on their farm in middle Tennessee. She loves to ride her horses, play with their dogs and relax on the porch, enjoying the rolling hills of her home south of Nashville. Country music is a passion of hers and she loves to listen to it while she writes.

She is an avid reader of romance novels and enjoys reading Nora Roberts, Jude Deveraux and Susan Wiggs. Finding new authors and delving into something different helps feed the need for literature. A registered nurse by education, she loves to help people and spread the enjoyment of romance to those around her with her novels. She loves cowboys so you'll find many of her novels have sexy men in tight jeans and cowboy boots.

Other books by Sandy

Love Me Once, Love Me Twice
Before the Night is Over
Two for the Price of One
Difficult Choices
Doctor Me Up
Country Minded Cougar
Gotta Love a Cowboy
Make Mine a Cowboy
Meet Me in the Barn
Stakin' His Claim
Taming the Cougar

The Call of Duty (Anthology)
Trouble with a Cowboy

Check out Sandy's website at
www.romancestorytime.com

Follow her on Facebook at
Sandy Sullivan
Twitter at sandys37

Secret Cravings Publishing
www.secretcravingspublishing.com